Star Girl

Star Girl

THELMA HATCH WYSS

Illustrated by John Pimlott

The Viking Press   New York

Copyright © 1967 by Thelma Hatch Wyss
All rights reserved
First published in 1967 by The Viking Press, Inc.
625 Madison Avenue, New York, N. Y. 10022
Published simultaneuosly in Canada by
The Macmillan Company of Canada Limited
Library of Congress catalog card number: 67–20962

Fic   1. Indians
      2. Idaho—Stories

PRINTED IN U.S.A. BY MONTAUK BOOK MFG. CO., INC.

For Pam

Contents

THE PEOPLE
OF THE SNAKE

The Bannock Indians of Idaho tell of a young girl of their tribe who talked to a star and disappeared into the sky. No one knows exactly how she went or where she went, just that she disappeared into the sky.

Perhaps this is what happened. . . .

Cousins

There were sunflowers—tall golden sunflowers with willowy bodies, tilting their sun-browned faces to the sky, bursting into song.

"Ee-dah-how. Ee-dah-how!"

The sunflower song stopped. Star Girl blinked, then opened her eyes to the morning.

There *were* golden sunflowers. There was a meadow lark somewhere singing, "Star Girl is a-pretty-little-girl." There was the muffled sound of the Great Falls in the background. And there was the brown face of her Shoshoni cousin, Only Child, laughing.

"Ee-dah-how," Only Child said again, pointing. There was the sun coming down the mountain. It was morning.

Star Girl pushed back the buckskin robe and sat up on her mat, hugging her knees for warmth. It would be long after the morning meal before the sun moved out from the shadows of the mountains to warm the valley floor.

"You win, again," she said to Only Child, sighing.

11

"You always awake before I do. Do you really sleep?"

"I don't watch the stars all night." Only Child laughed. "Come. I will help you with your mat."

Only Child had already taken her mat to the tepee. "I waited for you to go to the river," she said as she carried Star Girl's mat to the tepee.

Star Girl greeted her mother, Wise One, turning fish at the fire. Her two older brothers had eaten earlier and were fishing for more salmon below the Great Falls. The work for the girls that morning, Wise One said, would be repairing fish nets. "Work like a musk-rat before playing like a rabbit," she crooned.

Before working like a muskrat, however, there was always time for a splash in the cold waters of the Snake River. From a basket in the tepee the girls took their moccasins, their necklaces, and a porcupine-tail brush. They raced toward the river, jumping sage-brush, untieing their buckskin skirts as they ran.

Star Girl was the first down the bank of the river. Only Child could wake sooner than Star Girl, but Star Girl could outrun any short Shoshoni girl. Star Girl was Bannock—tall and slim as a sunflower.

Star Girl was proud to be Bannock. As long as she could remember, and as long as her mother, Wise One, could remember, their small tribe had lived peacefully with their Shoshoni neighbors, sharing hunting grounds

and camps along the Snake River plain at the base of towering snow-capped mountains.

Star Girl's favorite time was summer when the tribe wandered along the Snake River, a great water god lying on his back. Summer was gray campfire smoke drifting lazily into the sky, scenting the world with cedar and sage; summer was sleeping outside the tepee in sunflowers under a thousand silver stars; and summer was blue water—roaring down the mighty Snake, cascading down the black lava rocks of Great Falls, and trickling through ice-caked mountain streams.

Summer was not all play, though remembering during the long winter it seemed that way. At summer camps Star Girl worked at the side of Wise One, unloading the dog travois, securing the tepee poles, and rolling the long buffalo hides around the poles.

When her father, Tagee, and her brothers brought rabbit carcasses, she helped clean and dry the meat. In the Month of the Green Grass she dug in the meadows for camass roots until her knees were skinned, and in the Month of the Dry Grass she picked sarvisberries and chokecherries in the foothills until she was spattered with the red juice, looking like a big berry herself.

Work this summer seemed less like work than usual because Only Child shared it.

"We must bathe quickly," Only Child now shouted, ducking herself over and over again in the cold river water. Everyone shouted near the Great Falls. "The nets must be repaired before sundown."

There were always nets to be repaired at the Great Falls Camp. The young men fished from sunrise to sunset for the salmon which came upstream from the ocean. The water god of the Snake wanted all the fish for himself, so he tore the nets mercilessly. The women and young girls were kept busy repairing them.

The women had spent all day yesterday stripping bark for today's weaving from the willows up the river and had returned to camp with the darkness. For Star Girl and Only Child, yesterday had been a fine adventure. They had tried to get lost in the willows and then in the darkness, but nothing escaped the eye of Wise One.

"Stay near," she cautioned, glancing at the setting sun. "It is the time of the *Nin-num-bees.*"

Frightened, the girls followed closely the slow pace of Wise One until camp was in sight. Then feeling safe, Star Girl reassured her cousin. "The small people are not in the willows, but downstream near the Great Falls in the large rocks and caves. They will not snatch us here."

She took the hand of Only Child, however, remembering that although this was not the accustomed place of the Nin-num-bees, still one of those departed warriors might wander from the rocks and snatch her away in the twilight.

"Once," Star Girl whispered, "a young girl was picking berries alone when she saw a Nin-num-bee. She listened to his song and fell in love with him.

She followed him to his cave and was never seen nor heard of again."

Now in the yellow morning sunlight, though the rocks and caves were near, the fearful little Nin-num-bees seemed far away.

For a few minutes both girls sat shivering on the grassy bank, wringing their wet hair. Then Star Girl brushed her cousin's long black hair slowly, heavily with the porcupine-tail brush.

Star Girl liked her dark Shoshoni cousin. This was Only Child's first summer at the Great Falls. Her parents had permitted her to spend a summer with Star Girl's family because Only Child was lonely with no brothers nor sisters.

Wise One had smiled when she heard this, knowing Only Child was of marriageable age and that the tall, swarthy Bannock men were sought after.

"She will be welcome," Wise One had said. "We will treat her as our own."

Now the two brown girls listened to the loud drone of the waterfall.

"Tell me again the story of the falls," Only Child coaxed her cousin.

"Again?" Star Girl smiled. And she began, as her mother had begun time after time, the story of the Great Falls.

The Spirit Maiden

"Many years ago," Star Girl began, "the waters of the Great Falls were not so thunderous nor foaming. Your people, the Shoshonis, were camped here, and the men were preparing for warpath.

"One strong Shoshoni brave loved a beautiful young maiden of his tribe. Their last meeting was on the high rock that overlooks the plunging waters." Star Girl pointed, and Only Child stared at the jutting black rock.

Star Girl continued. "The brave went away, and the maiden came daily to stand on the rock to remember him.

"Many months passed. The young maiden's tribe returned up the Snake to Big Camp. But she stayed, and still came to stand on the high rock.

"One black night as she stood in her usual place, a warrior stepped out of the shadows and whispered to her. Then he disappeared.

"As quiet as stone, she stood for a long while, looking down into the deep waters like seething white teeth.

17

And then, slowly, she lifted her arms above her. She stood tiptoe for a moment, poised and beautiful. Then she dived in a long swift arc into the falling white foam."

Only Child sat as in a trance, her large brown eyes sorrowful. Then she turned her face from Star Girl so her tears would not show.

"The waterfall has never been the same since that time," Star Girl whispered. "And," she added mysteriously, "some say the spirit of the maiden can be heard crying from the dashing waters; and some say they have seen her spirit standing again on the high rock."

Star Girl began braiding her cousin's long dark hair. But how difficult Only Child made it. She kept turning her head toward the waterfall. It was not, however, the spirit maiden of the Great Falls that held Only Child's attention now. It was the young men fishing, their loud laughter and mock cries sounding above the constant din of the falling water.

"Your braids will be cockeyed today if you do not look straight ahead," Star Girl cautioned, jerking the braids into position. "They were a little cockeyed yesterday and the day before. Soon everyone will know your secret. Soon you will be known as Cockeyed Braids."

Only Child turned quickly into a stiff forward position.

After the hair braiding was completed, the girls tied on their buckskin skirts and sauntered back to camp. Two small gray birds ran frantic circles through the sagebrush, crying, "Killdeer, killdeer." Sunflowers swayed in the dry breeze.

"Do not tell," Only Child whispered. "I do not want to be called Cockeyed Braids."

"I will not tell"—Star Girl laughed—"if you promise to look straight ahead every morning while I braid."

Only Child promised.

Linking arms the two girls hopped into camp, telling everyone who would listen that they were twin jack rabbits joined together forever, looking for food— preferably roasted salmon.

In Camp

In the shade of the tepees the women and girls were bowed low over the fish nets. Soft doeskin robes covered their heads, hiding their faces.

"The old sun is kind," Wise One said. "He moves slowly across the sky." She rested her gnarled hands in her lap.

"Will he wait for us to finish the nets?" Star Girl asked.

"If we work quickly," Wise One cautioned, resuming her meticulous weaving. The nets whispered in her deft hands.

Occasionally there was an interruption in the low monotonous hum of the women and the dry whispering of the nets. A child cried and received attention; an old dog, too tired to hunt with the men, was shooed from the fish supply; a tall weary hunter returned, dropping his load at the feet of his wife.

Again came the low monotonous hum, the dry whispering. Star Girl and Only Child fidgeted. Their backs felt stiff.

"Listen to the day," Wise One said.

They listened.

Outside the camp was the day. From the sagebrush came the plaintive cry of the gray bird: "Killdeer, killdeer." The bark of a dog sounded far away, and an occasional faint shout from the fishermen below the falls floated into camp with the constant drone of the falls. A small wind was lost downstream in the deep caverns of the Snake.

"Where does the Snake go?" the girls asked Wise One.

"Far away to the end of all rivers."

"Have you been there?"

"No."

"Will you go there?"

"The falls are not higher at the end of the Snake, the little red flowers in its basin are not redder, and the berries near its banks are not sweeter. I will not go there."

"Where are the stars now?" Star Girl asked, looking at the blue sky. She stared into its depths trying to see the beginning.

"Asleep," answered Wise One.

"Your mother is very wise," Only Child whispered.

"Yes," Star Girl agreed, her small almond eyes looking deep into the far away, "but I would like to see for myself."

"When will we return up the Snake?" Only Child asked, thinking of her mother and father at Big Camp.

"Soon," said Wise One, "in the Month of the Dry Grass."

The low sound of the women began again.

"In the sky I see a great buffalo," Wise One said. "What do you see?"

"I see a frog."

"Two frogs."

They played the cloud game.

Finally the nets were finished. In one general movement the women rose and began making small fires. The sun dropped behind the Great Falls.

The fishermen returned to camp, yelling as if they were still below the roaring white foam, dropping salmon in colorful heaps. Star Girl's older brothers, Paseego and Commosie, were among the fishermen. They were tall and straight as trees. They strutted around camp with the other young men, teasing the dogs, and parading in front of the girls who were helping their mothers at the fires.

The hunters, who included Star Girl's father, Tagee, and little brother, One Arrow, returned with a variety of carcasses.

"Look what the great hunter brings," cried One Arrow, brandishing his rabbit carcass in front of Star Girl. "Next time I shall bring a bull elk," he said.

"A great hunter you are indeed," Star Girl said, laughing.

"We will take the great hunter fishing tomorrow if he doesn't hold on to the sleep too long," his older brothers teased.

Old Tagee sat near the fire puffing his pipe. Under his dark robe his tuft of hair, thrown backward from his forehead in Bannock fashion, showed wiry strings of gray. "A spirit found his arrow," he said, grunting.

One Arrow tagged his mother as she prepared the meal, explaining with gestures his hunt. Wise One nodded agreement to all he said.

After the meal of salmon and berries, cooking fires were left to flicker and die, and the families of the tribe gathered around a large fire in the center of camp.

Star Girl felt the excitement of the group. There would be wrestling tonight.

Names buzzed through the circle. A young man jumped into the center of the circle, throwing his buckskin shirt on the ground.

A cheer arose. *"Ah-hi-e. Ah-hi-e."*

Star Girl and Only Child squeezed through tall buckskin legs and squatted on the front row. The young man was Paseego. Star Girl felt proud. Only Child giggled.

Paseego stood defiantly a few minutes, then pointed to a bigger man in the circle. "Cameahwait!"

The group cheered.

The two men wrestled—grunting, crying, straining their ropelike muscles. Their bodies cast weird shadows in the dim firelight.

The contest was long. Bets were made. The cheering continued and rose to a piercing pitch.

Cameahwait slipped. He fell to one side crying, his forearm touching the dusty ground.

The onlookers laughed. Cameahwait laughed. Paseego laughed. All had enjoyed the game.

Paseego stood for a minute, tasting victory. Then he shouted for his next opponent.

After the wrestling, when the camp fire was very low, the old men told stories—stories of the Nin-num-bees hiding in the deep serpentine gorges below the Great Falls; stories of the *Tukuarikas,* the renegades from the Bannock and Shoshoni tribes who lived like animals in the high caves of the mountains, and who came in the night to steal from the wandering summer tribes.

Star Girl and Only Child crept closer to old Tagee, peering over their shoulders at the blackness of the night.

Women disappeared with babies into the black tepees; young children with drooping eyes were led like sleepwalkers toward the tepees. The old men smoked their pipes in silence.

The quiet darkness was violently interrupted. Two young men were arguing. A young girl, Little Moon, was dragged into the middle of the circle, crying with fright. The men contested for her in the dim firelight.

Tagee nodded his head at Star Girl and Only Child,

and they withdrew quickly and quietly into the darkness. They felt for their mats on top of the small basket in the tepee. They placed them together outside the tepee and crawled under the buckskin robes.

Then the haunting night noises began. The fire crackled mysteriously, low lullabies drifted from the tepees, the snore of an old woman stirred the softness, a serenade from an elderberry flute floated by, Little Moon whimpered pathetically from the circle of men, and the eerie howl of a coyote sounded far away—or was it so far away?

Perhaps the Nin-num-bees were wandering about. Perhaps the Spirit Maiden was calling from her foaming grave. Perhaps there was nothing in the darkness but a lonely coyote howling. Perhaps.

The noises of the night were sad and secretive. Star Girl, peering from under her buckskin robe, whispered shakily, "Do not fear, Only Child. The coyote is far, far away."

Up the Snake

It was the Month of the Dry Grass. The Snake River plain lay faded under the glaring sun, the sagebrush brittle, the willows listless. Pale sunflowers hung limp. A dry wind wailed over the land. Soon it would be time to return up the Snake to the high valleys.

"Today?" Star Girl asked impatiently.

"Today?" Only Child asked, anxious to see her parents again at Big Camp.

Wise One shook her head and continued pounding sunflower seeds into meal for porridge.

Then one day, suddenly, it was the day. Star Girl was roused from sleep early by Only Child. "Look," she exclaimed, "the men have started up the Snake!"

The men were leaving the camp, carefree, singing a shrill walking tune. A few rode fine Appaloosas, prancing as if on parade. But most of them, like Tagee, walked with their dogs proudly.

The women worked quickly. Like huge blossoms being plucked, the tepees collapsed to the ground. The pack dogs whined while the travois poles were secured.

27

Star Girl and Only Child helped Wise One roll the tepee and pack their few belongings on the two travois. Then they darted about camp, remembering mud pies and grass dolls in secret places that could not be left behind.

Finally the conglomerate procession moved. The loaded dogs with the women on each side ponderously filed into the dusty path of the men who now were toy figures in the distance.

As Star Girl looked back she felt a sadness. The home she had known for a while was now a barren spot on the desert. The fading sound of the Great Falls seemed lonely.

Near the trail Star Girl found a smooth pebble and held it securely in her hand. She would drop it at a medicine pile and in so doing drop her sadness.

"We will return next summer," Wise One said, sensing the melancholy of Star Girl. "Now we must follow the food. We go to Big Camp and then to Hot Springs, the place of your birth twelve years ago."

Suddenly Star Girl realized that Only Child would be left at Big Camp with her parents. "Will we camp at Hot Springs all winter?" she asked her mother.

"If the winter is very cold," she said, "we will return to Big Camp. And"—she smiled—"the winter will be cold."

Star Girl looked back a final time, then waved a lonely good-by to the vast emptiness.

As Star Girl walked in the dusty trail she wondered many things. She thought of the Great Falls and wondered if it stopped its barbaric roar when the tribe was not there to hear it; she wondered what the children of the Tukuarikas up in the high caves did all day long; she wondered if all the stars were asleep, or if, maybe, one were peeking, watching her.

The new stillness was frightening. Star Girl glanced at Only Child to see if her pounding thoughts were heard, but Only Child was staring quietly ahead, one hand on a dog's collar, her feet methodically moving.

The sun moved slowly across the sky. Star Girl's throat felt dry; her moccasins were covered with dust. Someone ahead began a low melody, and soon all the women and girls were singing.

Just as the sun dropped behind them, the men were

spotted ahead, waiting at the base of a large jutting lava rock. Near the large rock was a small medicine pile.

Little One Arrow ran to meet the women, waving a rabbit carcass and urging Wise One to prepare it quickly, for the great hunter was very hungry.

Star Girl walked the short distance to the medicine pile and deposited her pebble. Most of the sadness was gone now.

As the Bannock drew nearer each day to the high mountains they shouted in delight at the renewed color. Tall scarlet columbine and blue larkspur brightened the high meadows.

Star Girl and Only Child darted about, gathering armfuls of the brilliant flowers to cover the two dog travois. They entwined blue larkspur in their long dark braids, then blushed when Paseego and Commosie noticed.

Bushes in the foothills were laden with ripe berries, but only the young men ventured such a distance from the trail. Small patches of mountain maple had turned scarlet. A few quaking aspens had turned yellow. The scent of early autumn was in the air.

"I will bring you golden leaves from that bush way up there," Paseego bragged to the girls, pointing to the top of the foothills. He walked with a swagger.

"That high?" Only Child exclaimed, looking at the cluster of yellow bushes high on the mountain side. She shuddered. "You may meet the Tukuarikas!"

"I would like to meet the Tukuarikas!" Paseego said arrogantly.

All the afternoon Only Child glanced nervously toward the mountain as she slowly followed the trail.

"Do not fear," Star Girl told her. "He is Bannock." Star Girl was proud that her brother was high on the mountain, alone.

Just after dark Paseego slipped into camp, dusty and weary. He sought Only Child and dropped golden leaves at her feet.

Only Child felt a softness creep into her heart, but unable to meet the bold, proud gaze of Paseego, she lowered her eyes and stood shyly like a flower.

Paseego, however, felt her secret smile, and was happy.

Big Camp

They were ten days on the trail. The nights grew colder, each one turning other bushes on the mountain into flaming color. Star Girl and Only Child huddled together on one mat with the other over them for added warmth. They made promises in the night, too secretive for daylight.

"I shall never tell our secrets," Only Child whispered.

"Promise?"

"I promise."

"Promise to wear this necklace forever?"

"I promise." Only Child slipped the antelope-tooth necklace over her head.

There was a long votive silence, and then sleep.

The Bannock arrival at Big Camp caused much excitement. As soon as they appeared on the horizon, drums were beaten in welcome. Three Shoshoni riders on spotted Appaloosas rode to meet them.

The riders were very dark and very heavy-set, looking all shoulders on their prancing horses. The middle rider was arrayed in colorful skins, with a feathered

headdress that fluttered in the breeze. His robe of white ermine draped from his shoulders, across the back of the horse, down to the ground.

"It is Chief Ty," Only Child whispered.

Only Child stood anxiously near Wise One, peering into the faces of the short, dark Shoshoni women bringing water. One of the women noticed Only Child and put her arms around her.

"Where is my mother, Nan-nag-gai Woman?" Only Child asked.

The Shoshoni woman gave no answer.

Wise One, noticing Only Child's distress, gave permission for the two girls to leave her side.

They ran through the women, the children, the dogs, and the general clutter of the camp looking for Only Child's mother.

"Where could she be?" Only Child asked over and over. Then she saw her family's tepee. "Look!" she exclaimed. The tepee area was strewn with rubbish, emitting a rancid odor.

"My mother is ill," Only Child cried, running to the tepee. "Mother. Father," she called softly.

The growl of a dog answered her.

She flapped back the low door of the tepee and stood blinking at the darkness.

A fat Shoshoni sat facing the doorway, holding two lean, growling dogs, one on each side. Red wine dripped from paunch skins scattered around the floor. The dogs and the old Indian bared their teeth at the girls.

"Father?" Only Child whispered, creeping inside the tepee. "Nan-nag-gai, my father."

The old man hissed. His lean, yellow dogs growled again.

"Father," Only Child repeated. "It is Only Child, your daughter."

The old Indian loosened one dog who lurched at Only Child. "*Wah-ah!*" he sneered. The dog crept, snarling, toward the girls.

"Come," Star Girl whispered, offering her hand.

Only Child turned and staggered through the doorway. Then in a blind stupor, she fled.

The Bright Star

Only Child learned from a Shoshoni woman that Nan-nag-gai had gambled and lost his wife in a horse race to some passing Blackfeet. They had taken her east with them over the high mountains.

Only Child cut her long hair in grieving, and for many days she sat alone on the banks of the Snake.

Star Girl's family went to her. "You are my daughter now," Wise One said, wrapping her own doeskin robe around Only Child's shoulders.

"You are my sister," Star Girl said, smiling. She placed her new fringed moccasins on Only Child's feet.

Tagee and his sons observed in silence, looking very stern. But they were pleased.

Only Child felt less sadness now. She remembered something her mother had taught her. She said softly,

> Happily I shall greet the day;
> Proudly I shall walk my way.

"I will make you a hairbrush of your own," Star

Girl said excitedly, "if little One Arrow will catch me a porcupine."

"Catching the slow porcupine is women's work." One Arrow pouted.

Wise One quickly interrupted. "Tomorrow we go to the Hot Springs," she said. "One Arrow may soak in the hot pools."

One Arrow was happy again. The porcupine was forgotten.

All night Tagee, with the other men, feasted upon roasted mountain sheep and drank chokecherry wine. Then with five other Bannock men he led his family up a winding tributary of the Snake toward Hot Springs camp.

Hot Springs camp was at the mouth of a rugged canyon where high mountain streams rushing with melted snow joined to make the Portneuf River. At Hot Springs the river flowed peacefully through a mountain valley, secluded by high walls of lava rock, cedar, and pine. Tall trees dotted the valley near the river.

For a reason known only to the Great God, hot pools spouted along the banks of the Portneuf, pools which cured the sickness of the heart and made the body feel young again.

Two days from Big Camp the small group reached

a mountain pass, a natural entrance to the Hot Springs valley. The women in the rear heard the men's excited cries. *"Ah-ah-hi-e. Ah-ah-hi-e."*

"Hurry," Star Girl called to Only Child, who was lingering at a medicine pile.

Only Child dropped her stone, which made a faint eroding sound in the rocks, and walked slowly away.

Star Girl ran ahead, leaving Wise One with the two dogs. She rounded the sharp bend, breathlessly.

The valley walls were aflame with color—as if all the summer rainbows had been trapped at the canyon's mouth and draped over the high mountains. The ravines were dense with scarlet mountain maple. Golden foliage lined the blue river as it flowed from the canyon.

Star Girl gasped at the unexpected beauty and rushed back to tell Wise One and Only Child.

"Autumn has come early again," Wise One said, rounding the bend to see for herself. She adjusted her worn robe in weariness, but her eyes were bright. "Autumn came early like this twelve years ago when you were born," she said to Star Girl.

"This is my home then," Star Girl said. "We will return to Big Camp, and we will return to Great Falls, but this is my home, the beautiful place of my birth."

Before the sun dropped in the west, the women had made camp and had begun preparing the evening meal. The men lazily soaked themselves like logs in the hot pools. Star Girl's brothers left the pools occasionally to strut vainly about, but Tagee and the older men sat as if melting.

"I know a secret pool down the river," Star Girl confided as she and Only Child prepared their mats for sleeping. "I will show you tomorrow."

"The nights are too cold for sleeping outside the tepee," Wise One cautioned. "You will turn scarlet as the leaves on the mountains."

"Just one more night?" Star Girl pleaded.

Wise One hesitantly agreed, saying, "Little girls must learn."

The night was cold. The two girls snuggled together and peeked from their robes at the narrow sky between the mountains. A full moon shone down at them through the ragged skyline of pine. The stars seemed very bright in the cold night. A tune from an elderberry flute sounded softly, but very near. It was the courting tune of Paseego.

Only Child whispered, "One day I shall marry Paseego, your brother."

Star Girl squeezed her sister's hand in happiness for her. Then a great loneliness touched her. She looked at the brightest star far above her and whispered, "I shall marry that star up there." She had a strange feeling that the bright star heard, and smiled.

The Tall Tree

Early in the light of dawn the girls crept shivering inside the tepee. "We have turned scarlet as the leaves on the mountains," they whispered and cuddled to the warmth of Wise One, one on each side.

The girls rose with the sun and worked like muskrats at the side of Wise One. They made cakes from acorn flour, grasshoppers, and currants.

Soon Wise One said, "Now you may play like rabbits."

Star Girl said to Only Child, "I will show you my secret place now." She took the hand of her new sister and guided her through the sagebrush and rocks down toward the marshes of the river.

"Where is it?" Only Child asked breathlessly.

"Way down there." Star Girl pointed. "Come on."

Geese flew up from the tall grass, honking. The ground was soggy, and the girls made slurping sounds as they walked. They giggled.

"Look," cried Only Child, pointing to higher ground, "a porcupine!"

"Let's catch him," Star Girl whispered, "for your hairbrush."

The girls scrambled back up the gentle bank of the river and ran after the slow porcupine.

A tall golden poplar stood apart from other trees on the marshland. Its trembling leaves clattered in the breeze like falling raindrops. The porcupine scurried up its trunk.

"Stupid old thing," Star Girl exclaimed. "I will catch him for certain now." She scooped a little dirt into her hands, rubbed them together, and began climbing. As she climbed, the porcupine climbed.

"I just about have him," Star Girl called to Only Child, looking up at her from the ground. The golden leaves tickled her face and camouflaged the little spiny animal. "Where are you, you old porcupine?" she demanded, climbing higher.

A cry sounded from below. Star Girl looked down at Only Child, who seemed ever so small and looked ever so frightened. Star Girl had never climbed so high before. She looked again down through the golden leaves to Only Child, who was waving and crying.

"Come down, come down," she cried. "The tree has spirits. It is growing to the sky. Come down, Star Girl, come down!"

Star Girl began scrambling down the trunk, ignoring the snags and scratches. But as she scrambled down, the tree grew taller.

"Help," she cried. "Help me!" She called desperately to Only Child, a tiny figure far below her running away from the tree, then running back to beat upon its trunk.

Star Girl shook the branches around her, trying to stop the growing tree. She climbed downward until she was breathless, but the rocks, the tepees, and the Portneuf below became smaller, and the figure running back and forth became smaller still. The tree kept growing higher.

Star Girl loosened her arms to fall, but the golden leaves held her securely. She took a final look at the miniature world below, then lay her head against the fluttering golden leaves, and sobbed.

The tall tree grew higher and higher into the sky.

THE CHEYENNE OF THE SKY

The Land of the Sky

In the land of the sky, Star Girl stood dazed. Before her, as far as she could see, were grass-covered knolls dotted with clumps of low bushes and irregular mounds of rocks. Where she could no longer see the prairie, the sky began—blue and cloudless. She felt confused by the unfamiliar scene.

She turned in the opposite direction and saw more grassy knolls. They seemed smaller in the distance and became, far away, tiny hills against the blue sky.

Star Girl turned completely around, but the landscape was foreign to her. She turned slowly, then quickly. She wildly flung her arms, crying, "Where am I? Who am I?"

"Star Girl."

The voice startled Star Girl, and she turned quickly to it.

A young man stood a short distance from her. He stood motionless, strong as a wind-whipped bush on the knoll. He wore skin leggings and moccasins, but no other clothing. His thick black hair came to his

47

shoulders and then separated into little strings stuck together with pine gum. From one ear dangled a white bone earring. His black eyes held a steady, unrevealing gaze, but his mouth slowly formed a smile. He extended his hand to Star Girl.

"You are welcome here, Star Girl."

Though Star Girl felt the kindness of the voice, she drew back. She was afraid, yet she knew no reason for her fear. She looked at the young man helplessly.

He moved closer. "I am Norkuk," he said proudly, pointing to himself. "And you are Star Girl."

"Star Girl," Star Girl repeated, staring at her own moccasined feet, her brown legs, her skirt, and then at her open hands. "Star Girl. Star Girl. But who is Star Girl?"

Norkuk gently touched Star Girl's shoulder. "Come with me," he said softly. "You will be happy here soon. Follow me, Star Girl."

Norkuk turned toward the distant blue hills and began walking. He walked slowly up and down several knolls before he turned to look back. Star Girl was following. He smiled and walked on a little more quickly, a little more proudly.

As Star Girl followed around a rocky bluff she heard the barking of dogs and the shouting of children. Recognizing these sounds, she ran quickly around the rocks.

She saw children playing with balls, and dogs chasing and barking. In the distance near some trees was a camp with many lodges. She pointed excitedly. "My camp?"

Norkuk shook his head. "It is my camp," he said.

A little boy darted in front of them, chasing a rolling ball. He gave them a quick, shy grin. These were not her people, Star Girl knew. This was not her camp.

"Come with me," Norkuk said. He began walking toward the camp.

Like a frightened deer, Star Girl looked wildly about for a means of escape. But there was none.

Norkuk, ahead, paused and turned to her. Hopefully he repeated, "Come, Star Girl."

Again Star Girl followed blindly.

The camp was pitched in a broad flat area close to a small grove of trees. The lodges stood in a great circle, white under the sun. Paths led from all quarters of the camp—to the stream, to the corrals, to the woods. The paths were busy with people.

Near the camp Star Girl passed some women gathering sticks and digging roots. They looked up at her curiously. Between two knolls on a level area, young girls about the age of Star Girl were playing a game with long sticks. They were laughing and cheering.

Star Girl stopped to watch, but the girls were having too much fun to notice her. They were taking turns throwing long horn-tipped sticks. Most of the sticks when rested on end were twice as tall as the girls. The girls threw the sticks with an underhand throw, sliding them along the smooth, packed ground.

Star Girl's attention changed from the game itself to the girls. They were all slender and graceful, wearing dresses with many colors and designs. Rather than long braids hanging down their backs, their braids were coiled about their ears or doubled in a loop on their shoulders.

She turned from the girls to face Norkuk, who had walked back for her.

"*Ehyoestsimas,*" he said, pointing to the girls at play. "Throwing-stick game. I will make you a throwing-stick. The girls will one day cheer for you."

Norkuk crossed the path into the center of camp and skirted behind the lodges. On the far side was a path leading to the woods. In front of a lodge which was set a few feet outside the camp circle, he stopped. Soon Star Girl was at his side.

"Wind Woman will give you lodging," Norkuk said. "She is very old. She will like your help."

"Wind Woman is your mother?" Star Girl asked, frightened.

"Wind Woman is a grass-root woman," Norkuk said, pointing to the colorful, quilled designs on the lodge. "A medicine woman. She cures sickness." He pointed down his throat, coughed, then laughed.

"Oh," said Star Girl, still frightened.

Norkuk gave the shrill call of a bird, which startled Star Girl. Then he called, "Wind Woman."

From inside the lodge came clinking noises and the sound of slow, cumbersome movements. The door flap was pushed aside by a long root—or, Star Girl wondered, was it a hand?

"Stoop down," Norkuk urged, and Star Girl blindly obeyed.

"Do you have her, Norkuk?" a squeaky voice asked from inside.

Star Girl stared into the darkness. Fear gripped her. She knew she must flee. But as she turned, the rootlike hand, quick as a preying hawk, reached out and pulled her inside the dark lodge.

Guest or Captive?

Slowly Star Girl adjusted to her dark surroundings. She discovered she was sitting on the upper bench of the lodge floor staring into the ugliest face she had ever seen.

The face of Wind Woman was old. Wrinkles ran in deep furrows to a toothless mouth. The hair was white and gray tangles that seemed to sprout at irregular lengths from the head. A brown robe clasped by clawlike hands covered the hunched frame.

Wind Woman looked like the dark, shriveled roots about her. Her voice rambled incessantly, and Norkuk nodded as he listened. Hobbling to a workbench, she began pouring wine into three horn cups.

Star Girl trembled and Norkuk, noticing, laughed softly. "She is a bit strange," he said, "but she knows almost everything."

Norkuk's eyes shone with respect for the old grass-root woman. Still Star Girl did not drink from her cup until Norkuk had drunk fom his.

Star Girl looked around the lodge. Tall poles sup-

ported the conical skin walls. From one pole hung
skin bags of all sizes and colors, each marked with a
design or plant root, a claw or a horn.

What magic medicine those bags must contain, Star
Girl thought.

The bench on which she was sitting, she noticed,
continued around the lodge, higher than the general
surface of the floor. It was used for sitting and sleeping, and on the opposite side for food preparation.
Cooking utensils hung from a lodge pole. Baskets and
bowls were piled on the bench. In the very center of
the floor was a small, deeper excavation for the fire.

Star Girl looked up again to the medicine bags high

on the lodge pole. The bags were very small, each marked carefully—a red bead, an elk tooth, a rabbit paw, a spotted feather. Even the identifying features hinted of magical contents.

Wind Woman offered more wine. Though her eyes seemed kind, she still frightened Star Girl. Wind Woman urged her to drink, and because she was very thirsty, Star Girl drank another cup.

Wind Woman was pleased. "Juice of the elderberry," she said.

Star Girl smiled faintly. She had understood little of what the old woman had said, and her thoughts were jumbled. What is this place? How did I get here? Over and over the most frightening of all questions probed her mind: Who am I? Who is Star Girl?

Suddenly Norkuk pressed his hand to his cheek and gave a painful cry. Star Girl jumped, almost spilling her wine.

It was a joke, and Wind Woman and Norkuk laughed as if they had shared it before.

"What can you give me for my toothache?" Norkuk said to Wind Woman, indicating the little medicine bags on the pole which had fascinated Star Girl.

Chuckling, Wind Woman hobbled to the lodge pole and carefully took down a little bag marked with an elk tooth.

"Toothache medicine," she said, "from the crinkle-root plant."

"*Wah-ah-ah,*" Norkuk now cried, clutching his side, "arrow wound. I will die, Wind Woman. I will die. What can you give me now?"

"*Ah!*" Wind Woman chuckled again, dangling a small yellow bag. "I will give you little buffalo medicine from the windflower root. You will not die, Norkuk."

"Oh, but the wound is very deep," wailed Norkuk, still holding his side.

"Then I will mix medicine," Wind Woman said. "I will make a poultice." Her eyes quickly scanned her

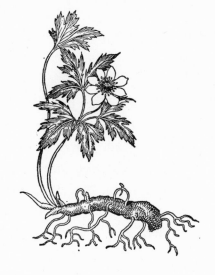

WINDFLOWER
(ANEMONE)

medicine bags, and she selected two from high on the pole. She pretended to mix the three bags together.

"To the windflower root I add some crooked medicine from the crooked root of the prairie ground-cherry; also I add a pinch of sweet medicine from the root of the hop vine. You cannot die now, Norkuk. I have cured your wound." Wind Woman was very pleased.

"I cannot die now," Norkuk admitted. "But my weary head aches." He held his head in his hands as if weeping with pain, but his dark eyes were sparkling with fun.

"That is because you talk so much," Wind Woman said. She shook a larger bag with five red beads on the outside. "Everyone talks too much," she said to Star Girl, indicating its large size. "I must always gather coyote medicine."

"Tell me," Norkuk said, pointing to baskets of roots, "which flower hides in her roots the headache medicine?"

Before Wind Woman could answer, Norkuk said, "I know." He grinned widely so his white teeth gleamed in the dim light of the lodge. "It is a secret. Wind Woman alone knows where to find the coyote medicine. But," he continued in a mock whisper, "if you get up before anyone else in camp and tramp in the woods all day long gathering roots for Wind Woman until your head aches, she will tell you the secret."

Wind Woman and Norkuk laughed. Carefully Wind Woman replaced the medicine bags on the lodge pole.

Star Girl felt that the acting had been mostly for her entertainment. She was fascinated, in spite of her misgivings.

"I shall go now," Norkuk said, rising from the bench, "but I will come tomorrow."

Wind Woman nodded and pressed his hand.

Norkuk motioned Star Girl to follow him outside the lodge. There, he asked, "You will stay here with Wind Woman?" It was a command.

Star Girl nodded in agreement, knowing no other choice.

"You will help her dig roots in the woods?"

Star Girl nodded again.

Norkuk placed his hand firmly on her shoulder and looked directly into her eyes. He stood two heads taller than Star Girl. "You may dig all roots but one."

Resentment flared within Star Girl. Who was this Norkuk? But more frightening, who was *she?*

"Do you know the red turnip?" Norkuk asked, his voice commanding.

"Yes," Star Girl said. She knew the root of the red turnip was good to eat.

"Do you know the black turnip?"

"Yes," Star Girl said, motionless. The black turnip had a root twice the size of the red turnip and was very difficult to dig.

"You must not dig the black turnip!" Norkuk was not the laughing boy he had been inside the lodge. His eyes were cold, his voice sharp.

Star Girl felt very much alone. She wanted to cry, but she continued to stare blankly at Norkuk.

Norkuk repeated slowly, "You must not dig the black turnip." He dropped his hand like a heavy weight from her shoulder, turned, and walked away.

Star Girl stood a long time before she stooped to enter Wind Woman's lodge. Am I a guest in this lodge, she wondered, or a captive?

The Forbidden Root

Star Girl awoke to the sound of the camp crier, an old man who rode a pinto horse inside the camp circle, shouting the commands of the chief, the order of the day, and personal news.

At first the crier's voice came as a droning shout, without words, but as he drew nearer his calls became distinct. Star Girl listened, but could understand only a few phrases. She thought, however, that the old man called her name.

Wind Woman, hunched over her workbench, ceased grinding roots a minute to listen. When the voice faded in the distance, she rose and began the housekeeping chores.

"I will get the water," Star Girl offered as Wind Woman reached for two paunch skins hanging near the door.

Wind Woman looked pleased. "Return the dead water first," she said, indicating the remaining water in the skins.

Star Girl followed several other girls and women to

59

WHITE BANEBERRY

the stream. Some looked at her curiously; some seemed not to notice.

Young boys were already playing along the stream —swimming, running races on the sandbars, and making clay images.

I know a wide river, a long river, Star Girl thought, staring into the water. But feeling sad and confused at the thought, she tried to forget it by watching the action about her.

Downstream, older boys and men practiced at shooting with their bows and sliding their slender throwing-sticks along the smooth ground.

Star Girl wanted to find the girls with their throwing-sticks, but she realized that most of the girls would be working. She returned slowly with the water to the lodge of Wind Woman.

For several days Star Girl carried water for Wind Woman and helped with work in the lodge. She decided that perhaps Wind Woman was not her enemy, but she still watched the old woman cautiously.

"We must go for roots now," Wind Woman said early one morning. She gave Star Girl a root digger, a short wooden stick whose point had been sharpened and hardened in fire. On the other end was a knob to protect the hand.

"*Hisso*," Wind Woman explained. She tossed a woven bag over her shoulder and motioned for Star Girl to do the same.

They walked north toward the wooded area. Women gathering sticks and bark and picking berries paused when they approached, and waved.

The ugly grass-root woman must be respected, Star Girl thought, feeling a new sense of pride.

They walked and walked until they were far from the other women and in another wooded area much thicker than the first. Wind Woman talked as they walked, pointing out the late autumn flowers.

"There are many roots to gather before snow falls," she said. Her sharp eyes noticed each flower.

"Hawkweed," she said, pointing to a clump of yellow flowers, "for snakebite."

"Should I dig it?" Star Girl asked.

"Another day," Wind Woman said. "I will not mix the roots while I teach you. Today we will dig only two flowers."

"You will teach me the magic of the medicine?" Star Girl asked, pleased.

"My magic is not the magic of the medicine man," Wind Woman explained. "My magic is knowledge, knowledge of the roots and grasses." She paused to examine a bough of berries.

"Then why can't the women gather their own roots if it is not secret magic which you do in the woods?" Star Girl asked curiously.

"Time, my *tsiso*. Time, my little one." Wind Woman chuckled. "My mother taught me for many, many years the medicine of the roots."

She pointed to a low flower with white berries tipped with red. "The white baneberry is poisonous. When women see me dig it, they dig it, and they become poisoned by it. I dig it and mix it as I was taught, and it is good medicine."

Star Girl kneeled by the curious plant. Tall spikes of berries, translucent-white tipped with red, sprouted from coarse green foliage. The white berries seemed to look back at her. "Doll's eyes," she exclaimed.

"Very poisonous doll's eyes," Wind Woman cautioned. "We will dig it later."

Wind Woman plucked here and there a leaf which she tucked in a pocket. She stepped carefully over fallen trees and small trickling streams. Star Girl followed at her heels.

"Here," Wind Woman called, pointing to a cluster of tiny white flowers. "Bird nests. We will dig them."

The dainty white blossoms on slender twisted spikes did not remind Star Girl of a bird's nest. She dropped to her knees, smelling the sweetness of the flowers.

"Are they poisonous?" she asked, watching Wind Woman carefully brush grass and leaves from the base of the plant.

"Not poisonous. Good for the stomach-ache and the fever," Wind Woman replied.

"Why are they called bird nests?"

"You will see. You will see," Wind Woman said, smiling.

Star Girl soon saw. Wind Woman held up the plant after digging it. The root was plaited together in such confusion that it looked like a bird's nest.

"I see a crow's nest." Star Girl laughed.

Wind Woman taught Star Girl how to thin flower patches so there would always be flowers in that place, and how to dig roots carefully so they would not be severed.

"The other flower will be harder to dig," Wind Woman said, coming upon a patch of tall purple-pink flowers swaying in the breeze.

"They are taller than we are." Star Girl gasped. "They look like pink smoke."

"The joe-pye weed," said Wind Woman, and she began explaining the medicinal powers of its roots.

Star Girl heard little of the instruction. She could only stare at the beauty of the massed fringed flower heads waving high above her head, reaching for the sunlight as it sifted down through the trees.

Star Girl and Wind Woman walked through the cool woods, spotting patches of the tall pink flower and the tiny white flower. The wood creatures sang and chirped and tittered.

The bag for the joe-pye weed filled quickly, but the one for the bird nests took twice as long to fill.

Somehow, Star Girl mused, here with the wild

JOE-PYE WEED

things, Wind Woman looked like a flower blossom instead of like the wrinkled, ugly root she had been reminded of a few days ago. Star Girl smiled to herself as she placed a bird nest with its roots in the bag. Even roots were becoming very pretty to her.

The sun dropped in the west. The root bags were filled. Star Girl and Wind Woman, walking slowly under their heavy loads, left the woods.

Star Girl sagged wearily under her heavy load and dropped it several times to the ground to rest. Finally, thinking she could continue no longer, she sank to the ground.

The spry Wind Woman paused, but she was accustomed to such loads and was anxious to return to her lodge. "Rest a while," she said to Star Girl. "The camp is in sight. You will not get lost."

Star Girl watched her hunched figure disappear and reappear as she walked up and down the grassy knolls.

The waving prairie grass looked like flowing water, Star Girl thought as she looked about her. She idly scanned the grassy area around her. Suddenly she stared at something a few yards from her—the coarse leaves of a black turnip were almost camouflaged in the tall grass.

Star Girl's heart pounded wildly as she remembered Norkuk's warning. "You may dig all roots but one. You must not dig the black turnip."

Star Girl hesitated and then walked over to the plant. Several clumps of it were scattered through the grass, almost choked by the thick growth.

Why must she not dig the black turnip? Why? What secret did its large root contain? Why should Norkuk forbid her to dig it? Why should Norkuk forbid her to do anything?

Star Girl dropped to her knees and began probing the hard ground with her hisso. It took some time to remove the thick grass around the plant, but soon Star Girl reached the cool dirt around its base. She worked rapidly, digging around the plant's deep, bedded root. She tried to wiggle the root to loosen it, but the plant stayed firm. Again she began digging, shooting dirt in all directions.

She stopped suddenly. A large moccasined foot stepped firmly on the hisso in her hands, holding it fast in the cool cavity of earth.

A Friend

Star Girl looked up into the stern face of Norkuk. She lowered her head expecting a blow, but there was nothing except cold silence.

Soon Norkuk removed his foot, but he said nothing.

Without looking up, Star Girl picked up the hisso and her bag of roots and walked swiftly toward camp.

Bitterness swelled within her. Why had Norkuk followed her? Why could she not dig the black turnip? Then the sadness came. Who was she? From what place had she come?

She dropped the root bag from her tired shoulders and dragged it the few remaining yards to the lodge of Wind Woman.

Near the door of the lodge were several objects which caught her attention—two pheasants, a bundle of twigs, and a little basket of blackberries. Leaning against the lodge was a tall red throwing-stick like the ones she had seen the girls using the day she had come to camp.

Star Girl admired the throwing-stick without touching it, assuming it belonged to a visitor inside the lodge. The stick was about six feet long and was stained a deep berry-red. One end was pointed with a white horn. As she examined it carefully she saw an inscription on the blunt end of the stick: *Star Girl.*

"Oh!" she exclaimed, clapping her hands in delight.

Wind Woman chuckled from inside the lodge, and her old wrinkled hand flapped back the door skin. "Norkuk was here."

"Oh." Star Girl hesitated. Then she took the throwing-stick in her hands and ran her fingers over it. "Norkuk," she said to herself. "I do not understand Norkuk. I do not really know Norkuk."

Darkness had crept into camp, so there was no time for trying the throwing-stick that day.

Star Girl and Wind Woman were just finishing their meal of roast pheasant and berries when they heard the sound of running feet and excited cries.

"My medicine bag," Wind Woman said, rising and pointing to a skin bag on the bench. Star Girl handed it to her.

Outside the lodge the frantic voice of the runner cried, "Grass-root Woman, Grass-root Woman. My baby has snakebite."

Quickly Wind Woman reached for two small medicine bags on the pole and dropped them into the larger bag. One was marked with a rattle from a snake and the other with small blue beads.

"Hawkweed and blue gentian roots," Wind Woman said. "Remember—hawkweed and blue gentian for snakebite. Come with me, Star Girl."

Many days passed and Star Girl found no time to use her new throwing-stick. She went each morning into the woods with Wind Woman and returned to camp with the darkness.

In the woods they dug the baneberry with white berries like doll's eyes. Star Girl counted twenty berries on one spike of the flower.

"Beautiful berries," she said. "Beautiful, poisonous berries." She carefully laid the plants in the root bag.

Wherever Star Girl looked she saw the tall joe-pye weed swaying in the breeze. "The pink smoke is everywhere," she cried, running toward the flowers.

As she ran she stepped on shorter flowers. "Flowers all over," she cried, stepping from white bird nests into a patch of yellow hawkweed. "There are too many flowers, Wind Woman. I cannot even walk!"

Wind Woman laughed. "Start digging where you are," she said. "It takes many, many roots for a small bag of medicine."

Wind Woman showed a new flower to Star Girl.

BLAZING STAR

The lovely blazing star. Its delicate pink blossoms looked like sparkling stars on the slender stalk.

"The roots of blazing star relieve the aching back and stiff knees," Wind Woman said. She chewed strings of this root as she gathered them.

Star Girl tasted a string, but spat it out quickly.

Wind Woman chuckled and continued chewing.

"What is this flower, Wind Woman?" Star Girl called, coming upon a flower with a strange little hood. It was streaked purple, brown, and green. Under the hood was a spike of scarlet berries. "Is it poisonous like the baneberry?" Star Girl asked.

"Not poisonous," Wind Woman said, "just good medicine. You have found the plant which gives the coyote medicine. It is the Indian turnip."

Many times while working in the woods Star Girl

asked Wind Woman, "What tribe are you? Do you know who I am?"

Wind Woman always answered, "We are Cheyenne."

"Am I Cheyenne, too?" Star Girl asked anxiously.

"You are Cheyenne now," Wind Woman said.

"But before that?"

The old grass-root woman never answered. Star Girl could remember nothing of her past.

Often on their return from the woods they found firewood and meat left by Norkuk at the lodge door. But they did not see Norkuk. And after spending a long day digging roots, Wind Woman often sat all night by the side of a sick child administering her medicine. One morning after such a night, she said, "I will not go to the woods today. I must rest."

"What work may I do for you, Wind Woman?" Star Girl asked.

Wind Woman smiled and nodded toward the long red throwing-stick. It had been placed near Star Girl's bed so she could see it before she went to sleep and first thing each morning. "You may play."

Now she could try the throwing-stick! Star Girl found a secluded spot to practice. Every time she threw the stick, its sharp point stuck in the ground a few feet from her. It had looked so easy when the other girls were throwing. In the afternoon she decided she might be able to glide the stick if she went to the smooth, hardened ground where the girls played regularly.

Star Girl approached the group of girls cautiously. No one seemed to object, so she stood at the end of the line of six girls to take her turn. All six girls sent their sticks a long distance, but one girl sent hers far beyond the others.

Star Girl remembered seeing her before. She was taller than Star Girl, and her braids were coiled around her ears. How beautiful she is, Star Girl thought.

Star Girl stepped forward for her turn. She gripped her red throwing-stick firmly, determined to send it

INDIAN TURNIP
(JACK-IN-THE-PULPIT)

at least as far as the other girls had sent theirs. She drew her arm back slowly, then brought it forward, and let the stick go. The stick bumped along for a few yards, then shot off the track into a group of children who were watching.

There was silence except for the squeals of the children as they dodged the stick.

Star Girl felt a sickness in the bottom of her stomach. She was the loser.

Two girls giggled. Then all six girls broke into loud laughter.

Star Girl stood as if frozen, wanting to run, not knowing what to do. Then, as if remembering something from long ago, she laughed.

They all laughed. The game had been fun for all.

The tall, slender girl retrieved Star Girl's throwing-stick and, still laughing, handed it to her. "It is a beautiful throwing-stick," she said. "I will show you how to throw it." She touched Star Girl's arm gently. "I am Little Heart," she said, her big brown eyes sparkling.

"I am Star Girl," Star Girl said with quivering lips. Two tears bolted down her cheeks. She had found a friend.

The Goldenrod and
the Aster

As often as she could Star Girl met Little Heart at the throwing track. Star Girl gradually learned the art of the game. She could send her throwing-stick for long distances, though not so far as Little Heart could. Nevertheless, she was delighted.

Little Heart told her of the Ehyoestsimas Contest for which all the girls were practicing. The contest was held once a year during the Month of the Big Hard Face on a track of ice. The throwing-sticks glided twice the distance on ice. Chief Two Elk himself conducted the games and stood at the one-hundred-yard line to judge. The winner was given a pony from the chief's own herd.

"I have dreamed of the pony every year," Little Heart confessed shyly. The two girls were walking along the track to retrieve their sticks.

"But who throws the stick farther than you?" Star Girl asked, surprised.

"Last year it was Red Bead Girl," Little Heart said, "but now she is no longer eligible."

One afternoon Star Girl gave Little Heart a small beaded medicine bag. "Violet roots," she said, handing it to her, "for pleasant dreams."

Little Heart opened the drawstring and poured some of the powder into her hand. It was black and musky —and magic! She wet her finger, stuck it into the powder, and put it to her lips. She smiled broadly, then offered some to Star Girl.

"We both shall have good dreams," Little Heart said. They laughed.

Another day while they were resting between throws, Little Heart asked, "Where was your home before Wind Woman found you lost in the woods?"

So that was what the camp crier had announced, Star Girl thought. Wind Woman had not found her in the woods. Norkuk had found her—out here on one of these knolls. The sadness crept around her, and she became very quiet.

"I remember nothing," Star Girl said sadly.

"I am sorry," said Little Heart. "Come to my lodge. I will show you my trinkets. You may keep the one you like."

The warm days of the Plum Month passed, and frost crept into the nights.

"We must go to the mountains before it snows,"

Wind Woman said often. Whenever they planned to leave, however, someone came crying, "Grass-root Woman, come quickly with your medicine."

One morning Wind Woman roused Star Girl from her bed before dawn. "Let us go to the mountains," she said. She scurried around the lodge like a little brown mouse, packing enough food for two days, but being careful to keep the load light.

Each one carried a large bag over her shoulders and a smaller one over her arm. Wind Woman wrapped an extra robe around Star Girl. Then quietly as night animals they walked in the darkness around the lodges and toward the eastern hills.

Wind Woman sang softly as she walked.

> *Ta-e-va na-ma-e yo ni-yi*
> *Tze-i-hu-tzit-tu na-ma-e yo ni-yi—*
> I go by night unseen on my way,
> Then am I holy—

Wind Woman's low crooning was barely audible. Star Girl listened carefully.

> *Tze-i-hu-tzit-tu he yo hi yo hi yo*
> *Hai yo ho yo Hai yo e yo e-e-yo.*
> Then have I power
> To make well the sick.

Over and over again Wind Woman sang the medicine song in the quiet darkness. Soon Star Girl joined in the singing.

When dawn came, Wind Woman and Star Girl were far from the camp. The sun rose blazing above the hills, and they walked with heads lowered to avoid its piercing glare. At noon the sun became a golden sunflower in the top of the sky. When the sun set in brilliant red in the west, the two weary travelers had reached the shade of the foothills.

"We are here." Wind Woman sighed, resting on a fallen tree.

Star Girl sank to her knees in a heap of golden leaves. She was too exhausted to speak. Wind Woman

BLUE GENTIAN

covered her with her robe and more golden leaves. She slept.

Star Girl awoke to a golden world—golden leaves were falling on her face, goldenrod on tall stems waved like beautiful wands, yellow sunflowers nodded their heavy heads.

Sitting up and rubbing her eyes, Star Girl saw more flowers—blue flowers, like patches of sky in the golden world. Blue gentians were blooming as if determined to change the golden world to blue.

"Oh!" Star Girl cried. She ran from golden flower to blue flower shouting with delight.

Wind Woman appeared from the thick brush. "Here are blackberries for breakfast. Then we will dig the beautiful blue gentian."

Star Girl had seen the powder of the gentian roots which had cured the baby's snakebite, but she had never seen the beautiful blue blossom of the flower.

"You are too beautiful to dig," she whispered to the blue flowers. "I shall save every blossom and take you home to my friends—Little Heart and . . . and maybe . . . Norkuk." She thought of Norkuk often since he had left the throwing-stick, but she had not seen him since the day she had tried to dig the black turnip.

Star Girl kneeled among the flowers, opening her arms as if to embrace all of them. Her long braids brushed the blossoms.

Then Star Girl noticed another patch of blue in the golden foliage and ran there. Again she kneeled among the lovely blue blossoms. "You are too beautiful to dig," she exclaimed.

Wind Woman, picking blackberries, chuckled. "We will not dig the blue aster," she said. "Come now, and eat some berries."

All day Wind Woman and Star Girl worked. Before the darkness came all the root bags were bulging.

"Why didn't we bring more bags?" Star Girl asked, bursting with enthusiasm.

"Can you carry more?" Wind Woman asked, smiling.

When darkness came they sat on their bed of leaves, watching the small fire Wind Woman had made. The darkness was cold.

Wind Woman poked at the fire nervously. "We must leave before dawn—before the snow comes," she said. She drew her robe more tightly about her old shoulders and mumbled into the fire.

Star Girl drew closer to Wind Woman, and as she stared into the fire and listened to the noises of the night, she seemed to remember another fire with people laughing and shouting around it. She stared sadly, for she could remember only the fire.

Wind Woman stirred the ashes. "You noticed the blue asters growing among the goldenrod?" she asked. "They are sisters. I will tell you a story."

"Long ago in a tribal war," Wind Woman began, "an Indian village was destroyed. Only two little girls escaped. They made their way through the woods to a very old grass-root woman who lived beside a creek, gathering plants all day long. So old and so learned was she that the Great God bestowed upon her magical powers.

"The grass-root woman welcomed the little girls. One wore a fringed doeskin dress dyed the color of bright gold; the other wore a dress of pale blue."

Wind Woman paused for several minutes. Only when Star Girl stirred did she go on with her story.

"The old grass-root woman looked into the future and saw no happiness for the little girls."

Wind Woman paused again and poked the fire.

"What happened, Wind Woman. What happened?" Star Girl asked impatiently.

"At night," Wind Woman continued in low whispers, "when they lay down to sleep on the grassy banks of the creek, the old woman covered them with leaves and sprinkled them with a magic powder.

"The next morning only two flowers were there—
one a bright yellow goldenrod, still showing the doeskin fringe, and the other a pale-blue aster."

Wind Woman stared quietly into the fire.

Star Girl wondered, watching her, if perhaps Wind
Woman had been the old grass-root woman in the
woods who had changed the little girls to flowers.

"It is a beautiful story, Wind Woman," Star Girl
said. "It is a sad story."

As she lay curled in her bed of leaves Star Girl
wondered if, perhaps, awaking in the morning she
would be a beautiful flower instead of Star Girl. She
shivered under her robes.

The snow came before dawn. The two sleepers were
covered with several inches of the whiteness when they
awoke, and it still came down heavily.

"We cannot go now," Wind Woman moaned. "We
must wait until the snow stops falling." She built a
fire which sputtered several times and then went out.

Wind Woman and Star Girl sat huddled in their
robes, leaning against a tree with the root bags over
their feet. They divided a small cake and then sat
quietly watching the bushes and flowers turn into
strange white designs.

"Will it stop soon, Wind Woman?" Star Girl asked,

feeling cold and hungry. She wished Wind Woman would work some real magic.

"The first snowfall is usually brief," Wind Woman said. "Do not fret. It will stop soon."

But the snow continued falling. It fell straight down for a few hours; then a wind came and blew the flakes into whirling circles. Wind Woman again built a fire which struggled for a while against the storm, but soon sputtered and died.

Wind Woman walked a short distance into the whirling whiteness. She returned, shaking her head. "We could not walk in the snow for long. It is too soft, too deep."

The snow fell all afternoon. Star Girl grew sleepy and dropped her head against the warmth of Wind Woman.

"We must not sleep," warned Wind Woman, shaking her. "If we sleep, we die."

But Star Girl did not care. She could not keep her eyes open longer. Wind Woman may change me into a beautiful flower, she thought as she dozed.

She awoke to a cry—a distant cry. The snow had stopped falling. Darkness was settling over the white world. All the strange forms around her seemed to move. She reached for Wind Woman, but Wind Woman was gone.

Again she heard the strange cry. Was it the cry of a coyote? There was another cry, answering the first. The coyote was not alone.

Star Girl reached for a stick to probe the ashes of the fire, then held the stick motionless. She stared into the gathering darkness, seeing strange dark forms. Four dark forms were moving slowly toward her.

Norkuk

The dark forms were Norkuk with two horses and Wind Woman. She had heard his call and walked to meet him.

Star Girl cried with relief. At first she did not know Norkuk. Covered with fur from his head to his feet, he looked like a big brown bear. But she was glad it was Norkuk.

Norkuk wrapped Wind Woman and Star Girl in dry robes, rubbing their hands with his to warm them. As he worked he scolded Wind Woman for leaving so secretly in the night without taking one of his horses.

Wind Woman mumbled indistinctly.

"We must go now," Norkuk said, "while the horses know the trail."

He lifted Wind Woman on one horse and secured the root bags behind her. He mounted his pony, then held his hand for Star Girl to mount behind him.

The horses turned west in the clear cold night. All was silent except the crunching of their hoofs in the new snow.

Star Girl leaned against the broad, warm back of
Norkuk. Her eyelids were heavy. *"Pi laya kia.* My
thanks I give you," she said softly.

"Pi laya kia," she said again, "for this, and"—she
paused a moment—"for the beautiful throwing-stick."

"Ha-ah!" Norkuk urged the horses forward. He sat
very tall on his black pony.

Star Girl's throwing-stick went twice the distance
on ice that it did on the dirt track. "Oh, I shall be the
champion at the contest," she cried, teasing Little
Heart. She ran along the edge of the ice track after
her throwing-stick.

"Watch this!" Little Heart called. She sent her yellow stick gliding over the ice. It passed the red stick. "I shall be champion," Little Heart cried, running to retrieve her stick. Both girls laughed.

Each afternoon the girls practiced. Each afternoon Little Heart's stick passed Star Girl's red stick by a few yards. Soon the distance became shorter. Once Little Heart's yellow stick stopped several feet behind the red stick.

Both girls stared in disbelief. Then they retrieved their throwing-sticks and walked back to camp in silence.

Could it be possible? Star Girl wondered, grinding roots in the lodge. Could it be possible that my throwing-stick might pass Little Heart's stick in the contest? She had assumed Little Heart would be champion. Little Heart deserved to be champion; she had taught Star Girl the art of throwing.

Star Girl stopped grinding the stringy tansy roots which Wind Woman had gathered during the summer. Now in the winter the old people were asking for the sore-muscle medicine.

Star Girl could imagine herself accepting, amid cheers from the entire village, the beautiful pony from Chief Two Elk. How she would love that pony! But most of all, she could hear the call of the old camp crier, *Star Girl, champion of the Ehyoestsimas Contest*. Then she would be someone. Then she might know who she was.

And Little Heart? Star Girl looked into the bowl of dried roots and slowly began rotating the bone maul. She did not want to imagine the disappointment of her friend. She pressed the maul heavily against the inside of the bowl, making dull sounds.

"Wind Woman, Wind Woman." It was Norkuk's voice.

Wind Woman smiled and motioned for Star Girl to open the door flap. Wind Woman spent many hours on her bed, sipping a tansy brew. Her bones felt very old since the snow had fallen.

"Wind Woman says you may come in," Star Girl called. She smiled at Norkuk as he entered the dim lodge.

Norkuk had firewood, which he dropped near the door. He removed his fur cap and gloves, and blew into his hands to warm them.

By the golden light of the fire, they drank warm elderberry wine. They talked of many things—the deep snow, Norkuk's latest grouse hunt, the Ehyoestsimas Contest.

"Most of my friends are betting on Little Heart," Norkuk said, sipping the red wine.

Star Girl said nothing, but stared into the flickering fire. There was a long silence. Star Girl could feel the dark eyes of Norkuk looking at her.

"You will still compete?" Norkuk asked her.

Star Girl looked at Norkuk and thought of the beautiful red throwing-stick he had given her. She thought of her friend Little Heart. Could Norkuk know the conflict within her heart? She pictured him standing with his friends at the contest, cheering for her and the red stick. She knew what she must do.

"I will compete," she answered.

Norkuk was pleased. "May the red stick bring you luck," he said.

The Elderberry Tune

"Wind Woman, Wind Woman." Again, it was Norkuk.

Wind Woman nodded, and Star Girl opened the door flap.

Norkuk carried snowshoes, which he leaned against the side of the lodge. His black dog waited outside.

"It is the Month of the Big Hard Face," Norkuk exclaimed, "and the snow is deep on the ground."

Wind Woman chuckled and rose from her bed, where she had been grinding roots.

"Is it not the time of the yellow witch? *Inajan we.* Rise up, Grass-root Woman. Let's go into the woods."

"A yellow witch in the woods?" Star Girl asked. She began wrapping herself in outdoor furs.

"We will show you," Norkuk said. He reached for snowshoes hanging high above the door opening.

Norkuk and Wind Woman skimmed the snow easily in their snowshoes, but Star Girl walked like a clumsy bear. They all laughed. The black dog followed, crisscrossing their wide trail.

They entered the silent woods. Trees were bowed with heavy snow, and the withered flowers incased in ice made strange, lovely patterns. A few dry red berries clustered on trailing branches. Only a crow cawing from its roosting place broke the white stillness.

"*Le lela wasté.* This is beautiful," Star Girl exclaimed.

Norkuk and Wind Woman smiled.

"Wait," Norkuk said, "until you see the yellow witch."

They glided carefully through the winter patterns. Then, suddenly, they saw it, all at the same time.

"*Tsitoni toyus!*" Norkuk cried. "Look!"

But Star Girl was already staring at the straggly bright-yellow blossoms of the tall shrub. They looked like fingers curling. "Oh," Star Girl cried, "the beautiful fingers of the witch."

"Gather its bark and twigs for liniment," Wind Woman instructed Star Girl and Norkuk. "The time of the witch hazel is also the time of the *pavame* tree. I will find it and gather its roots for the fever."

Wind Woman found the newly budded sassafras tree nearby. She nibbled its green buds as she dug in the snow for its roots.

A noisy crow flew back and forth between them, scolding.

The day of the Ehyoestsimas Contest was cold and clear. The track had been flooded, and the cold nights had turned the water to ice.

It seemed to Star Girl that everyone in the village was gathered along the ice track. The old men sat on prancing horses, rearing and whinnying for free rein; the young men galloped their horses along the track, making them shy near the girls and women sitting on logs. The women squealed and ducked beneath their heavy robes. Laughing children, ignoring threats from their mothers, pulled howling dogs over the ice.

Even Wind Woman set aside her work, and bundled like a great white bear, joined the women on the logs.

When everyone was assembled and the ice track cleared of children and dogs, Chief Two Elk rode swiftly to the track on his white horse. His Chief's headdress glimmered in the sunlight. His long white robe draped over his horse and rippled over the new snow. The crowd cheered as the Chief stationed himself at the one-hundred-yard line to judge the contest.

Forty-five girls stood in line for the first competition.

"Where did all the girls come from?" Star Girl asked Little Heart. She knew only a few.

"Do not worry," Little Heart said. "They have been practicing in their lodges. They will not throw far."

Still Star Girl nervously gripped her throwing-stick.

"Do not let your arm get stiff," Little Heart cautioned.

Star Girl loosened her grip, and peered into the crowd. Norkuk was there, near his friends, sitting tall on his black pony, looking very much like a chief. When she looked at Norkuk, Star Girl felt she must win.

The drums sounded. "Poom, poom, poom." An official on a gray horse called the name of the first contestant.

The girl stepped to the head of the line, removed her fur jacket, and gracefully threw her long throwing-stick. The stick glided smoothly over the ice, but stopped before reaching the one-hundred-yard line.

"Seventy-five yards," called one of the men stationed along the track.

Three other girls had turns. Two girls sent their throwing-sticks to eighty yards, and one girl sent hers sailing from the ice into the spectators. Then the name of Little Heart was called.

Star Girl watched her friend remove her heavy jacket and secure her foot position. Then with one smooth throw Little Heart sent her yellow stick gliding past the one-hundred-yard line.

Chief Two Elk raised his arm high over his head. The crowd yelled.

"One hundred twenty-five yards," an official called when the yellow stick came to a stop.

When Star Girl looked at the happy face of Little Heart, she knew that she, Star Girl, must not win.

Star Girl was called next. Like the girls before her, she removed her jacket, stood for a moment, and then with all the strength of her body sent the red throwing-stick over the ice.

The red stick passed the fifty-yard line, the seventy-five-yard line, and then the one-hundred-yard line.

Chief Two Elk raised his arm again.

The spectators cheered and pressed over the boundary lines of the track.

Star Girl strained to see where the red stick stopped, but she could not see. Had her stick passed the yellow one? Could she perhaps win the contest? Star

Girl's heart pounded wildly as she waited for the call.

"One hundred fifteen yards," called the official. The red throwing-stick had not passed the yellow stick. Little Heart had won the first competition.

Little Heart, Star Girl, and three other girls were eligible for the second competition. The girls drew lots for position in line. Voices from the crowd grew higher and higher over the booming drums as bets were made.

Star Girl drew first position. When her name was called, she stepped forward. The ice glittered like a thousand silver stars.

"Make it one hundred twenty-five!" a voice called from the crowd.

"For three buffalo skins," called another.

"Quiet, so she can throw," came from another.

Star Girl felt very much alone. I must win, she thought. I must be someone! She drew her arm back slowly, then thrust it forward with all her strength, and let the red stick go. "Please, red stick, go far," she whispered.

"Fifty yards. One hundred yards. One hundred twenty-five yards. One hundred forty," the official called. The red stick had never sailed so far. No other throwing-stick in the second competition, not even the yellow stick, reached it.

Above the booming drums, an official announced the finalists. "Little Heart of the lodge of Big Heart, and Star Girl of the lodge of Wind Woman."

The crowd cheered.

Star Girl and Little Heart waited impatiently for their throwing-sticks to be returned.

"There will be feasting and dancing before the final throw," Little Heart shouted over the beating drums. Then with a quick laugh she added, "What magic did Wind Woman put on your throwing-stick?"

Their throwing-sticks were returned then, so Star Girl gave no answer. The tension between them made her uneasy.

"You go ahead," Star Girl said. "I will look for Wind Woman."

Little Heart hesitated, but was pulled forward by

some cheering friends. She waved her hand quickly and was lost in the crowd.

Star Girl waited a few minutes, then walked to the lodge of Wind Woman. Wind Woman was there already, adding logs to the fire.

"Warm yourself," Wind Woman said. "Then get some sleep." She sat at the foot of Star Girl's mat. "I will not let you sleep too long," she said.

Star Girl lay on her mat, but she did not sleep. She wondered. She wondered if she might be the winner of the contest. If so, would she lose the friendship of Little Heart? If she lost the game, would she lose Norkuk's friendship? Star Girl tossed on her mat.

Late in the afternoon the drum signal for the contest sounded throughout the camp. Star Girl rose quickly and reached for her throwing-stick.

Wind Woman hobbled to her feet, mumbling about her old bones. "Remember it is just a game," she said. Then she took Star Girl's hands in her own. "You will be gracious if Little Heart wins the contest?" she asked.

Star Girl looked into the wrinkled face of Wind Woman. She felt a great love for her. "I will be gracious," she said.

Wind Woman continued, "You will be gracious if Star Girl wins?"

"I will be gracious if Star Girl wins," Star Girl repeated. She put her arms around the humped form of
Wind Woman and hugged her. Together they walked
to the ice track.

The afternoon sun was warm. Discarded fur hats
and jackets were flung along the ice track and in piles
near the logs where the women sat. The drummers
had removed their buckskin shirts and sat, bare-
chested, beating their heavy drums.

The drums stopped. Chief Two Elk rode to the
track, swiftly, on his prancing white horse. Behind
him trotted a frisky white colt.

The white colt. White as new snow under the sun.
Star Girl rested her throwing-stick on end and smiled
at the pony.

There were cheers from the crowd. And calls.

"There's only one colt!"

"And one winner!"

Little Heart chattered at her side. "It's the best pony
ever. My arm is so tense I'll never be able to throw
far. Where were you during the feast?"

Star Girl heard only the trotting hoofs of the white
pony on the hardened snow. She saw only its tossing
head and flowing mane.

The third competition took just a few minutes of
the long, long day. Little Heart threw her yellow stick

first, and then Star Girl threw her red stick. Both sticks passed Chief Two Elk at the one-hundred-yard line.

There was a hushed silence as the Chief rode his prancing horse onto the ice. He dismounted like a flash of brilliant rainbow and held up the winning stick.

"The winner at one hundred forty-five yards," he called. It was the yellow stick.

The cheering of the crowd was loud.

Star Girl stood for an instant bewildered, alone. The faces of the crowd blurred before her. Then she noticed the face of Wind Woman, distinct in the blur of faces, and she remembered.

Star Girl touched the arm of Little Heart, who was also standing for a moment, alone. "I am happy for you, Little Heart," she said.

"You are my dearest friend," Little Heart whispered.

The drums beat loudly as Chief Two Elk rode toward the starting line leading the white colt.

Star Girl stepped back into the crowd, but Little Heart reached out for her. "We shall ride the white pony together," she said.

The drums beat louder, the rattles crackled, and the cheers rose higher. Little Heart bowed low before the majestic Chief.

Lying awake in her bed, Star Girl pondered the activities of the day. I am not Star Girl, champion of the Ehyoestsimas Contest. One day I will know who I am. I *must* know who I am!

She heard the sound of footsteps outside on the crusted snow and sat up. Who needed Wind Woman's medicine tonight? But as Star Girl reached to wake Wind Woman she realized the caller was not for the grass-root woman. Low notes of an elderberry flute filled the hushed night. It was the courting song of Norkuk.

Star Girl blushed and lay back quickly on her bed. She hoped that Wind Woman did not hear, yet she knew that she had.

When the melody stopped, the night seemed very still. Soon the footsteps faded away.

"I am not Star Girl, champion of the Ehyoestsimas Contest," Star Girl whispered in the quiet night. "But I am Star Girl, best friend of the champion Little Heart; Star Girl, assistant to respected Grass-root Woman; and"—she hoped Wind Woman could not hear the drum pounding inside her—"Star Girl, favorite one of Norkuk."

A great happiness filled her heart.

An Invitation

Spring came suddenly.

One day Star Girl saw one lonely bluebird search-
ing for a dry place in the thawing snow. The next day
there were many bluebirds, chirping gaily as they built
their nests.

One day she saw one blossom of blue-eyed grass,
and the next day the wide prairie was blue. A single
yellow flower burst from the goldstar grass, and the
next day the blue prairie was dotted with gold.

Children ran up and down the knolls shouting, for-
getting warm jackets. Their mothers ran to Wind

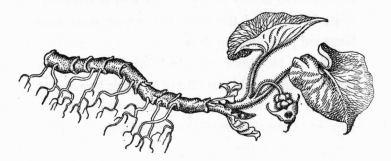

SNAKEROOT (WILD GINGER)

Woman for cough medicine. Wind Woman prescribed dandelion tonic for everyone in the village.

Wind Woman and Star Girl went every morning to the woods. The golden sun warmed the old bones of Wind Woman, making them limber again.

The roots of spring were rich with medicine. From beneath the dead leaves of winter, snakeroot lifted its red bell-like flowers; the purple windflower raised its pale blossoms on slender stalks above the melting snow.

Wind Woman taught the medicine of the spring roots to Star Girl: snakeroot for snakebite, windflower for arrow wounds, poisonous May apple for the ailing liver, squawroot for sores, the moccasin flower for nerves, and yellow goldstar for the stomach-ache.

Star Girl gazed in wonder at the masses of short golden buttercups. How could such pretty little flowers have roots of deadly poison? She stared at the lovely white blossoms of the bloodroot, whose roots gave bitter red juice used for dyes.

"Dig the bloodroot carefully," Wind Woman cautioned. Then she told Star Girl of its magic love charm. A young man need only dip his fingertips in the red juice and leave their imprint on a girl's cheek, and no girl could resist him.

And violets.

"Do not hide from me, little violets," Star Girl said, digging in the damp leaves and grass. "Your precious roots bring delightful dreams. Did you know?"

"And you—" She pointed to a cluster of white lacy flowers. "The roots of bird nests make any dream, good or evil, come true. Did you know that?"

Wind Woman and Star Girl journeyed again to the eastern mountains, this time riding two of Norkuk's horses.

The hillside was covered with large purple blossoms. "Oh," Star Girl exclaimed, "a whole mountain of flowers!" She ran with open arms through the flowers.

"Now the robins know that spring is here," Wind Woman said.

Star Girl kneeled and buried her face in the blossoms. She jerked back quickly, her nose wrinkled. The scent of the flowers was not pleasant.

Wind Woman laughed. "It is the wake-robin," she said. "Spring is truly here."

The old camp crier's news, whatever it was, was creating much excitement in camp. Star Girl lifted back the door flap to listen, but, at the motion of Wind Woman, let it fall. She continued bagging roots.

"You will hear soon enough," Wind Woman said, hooking a large bag of cranesbill roots to a lodge pole.

She attached one of the gnarled rootstocks on the outside to identify it. "Extract from cranesbill roots makes fine salve," she mumbled as she worked.

Star Girl did hear the news soon.

The camp crier stopped in front of their lodge and announced, "Chief Two Elk invites the maiden Star Girl to the annual Feast of Maidens . . . to be held at the stone altar the day after the new moon . . . before the sun reaches the middle of the sky."

The crier rode on calling, "Only pure maidens are invited . . . Chief Two Elk also invites parents and young men to be present to see that no unworthy maiden joins the feast. . . ."

Star Girl jumped from her bench and hugged Wind Woman. Her dark eyes sparkled.

"It is a great honor to be invited," Wind Woman said. "You have been watched, voted upon, and chosen as one of the fine young women of the village. At the feast you will declare your purity and vow to remain pure until you marry. The finest young men will court you. You will be respected and honored and may marry the one of your choice."

Star Girl listened carefully as Wind Woman continued in solemn tones.

"At the feast any young man is permitted to challenge any maiden whom he knows to be unworthy. Some challenge a girl because she has rebuffed them, but woe to him who cannot prove his case." Wind Woman shook her head dolefully.

"What would happen?" Star Girl asked.

"Perhaps death," Wind Woman said.

Star Girl shuddered. She hoped she would not be challenged at the feast.

"Do not worry," Wind Woman said. "I will coach you well. And that day I will be seated in the chaperons' circle." Wind Woman seemed as delighted as if she were a young girl herself.

Star Girl could not imagine Wind Woman as a young girl; it seemed to her that the grass-root woman must have always been an aged, white-haired woman. Had she ever taken vows at the Feast of Maidens or been courted by a young man?

Star Girl watched the old woman slowly move to a long basket and carefully remove a folded dress. She placed it on Star Girl's lap.

The dress was soft buckskin, white as snow. It was fringed and heavily quilled. Star Girl had never seen a dress so beautiful. She stared from it to the delighted Wind Woman, who was clapping her hands and dancing a jig around the lodge.

"Do you like it?" Wind Woman asked.

"Is it really mine?" Star Girl asked timidly. "To wear to the feast?"

Wind Woman nodded. "It was made by Norkuk's mother, The Quiller."

Star Girl laid the white dress on the bench and hugged Wind Woman. "Pi laya kia," she said.

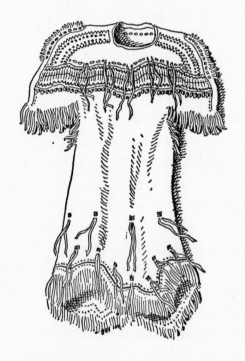

The Feast at the Red Altar

Star Girl rode with Little Heart on her white pony to the feast site. The pony walked as if nothing at all exciting were happening. Star Girl wanted to jump from the pony, and skip and dance all the way to the red altar.

It was the white quilled dress. Ever since Wind Woman had given the dress to her, Star Girl had been skipping and dancing. The dress was beautiful. It made her beautiful.

Earlier, in the lodge, Star Girl could hardly sit still long enough for Wind Woman to decorate her hair. "If you don't sit still," Wind Woman had cautioned, "the bloodroot will spill on your dress."

Wind Woman slowly painted the central part of Star Girl's hair bright red with the bloodroot. Then she painted her smooth brown cheeks.

Star Girl thought Wind Woman would never finish. She sat patiently, however, afraid to move until the bloodroot was dry.

Then Norkuk had brought the white moccasins—

107

white quilled moccasins! Never again would she walk. She would dance forever!

She skipped out of the lodge and down to the stream. She kneeled on the grassy bank and looked down into the clear water.

"Oh!" she exclaimed. She was beautiful. She looked a long time.

Then there was another beautiful face in the water —a beautiful face with red cheeks and a red part in her hair too. It was the face of Little Heart.

Star Girl looked up and saw Little Heart kneeling on the grassy bank. She wore a yellow quilled dress. Both girls smiled broadly, then walked arm in arm back to camp.

Now they rode the white pony together, trying their best to act as their chaperons wanted.

Wind Woman, dressed in a tan buckskin dress, rode one of Norkuk's ponies. At her side rode Little Heart's mother, Fire Bug, and Norkuk's mother, The Quiller. Wind Woman and Fire Bug carried wooden bowls to use during the ceremony. The women talked faster than usual; they had spent many days preparing for this occasion.

Other girls came on horses, some on foot. All were dressed in their finest clothes. They gathered shyly around the large cone-shaped rock, watching the spectators arrive.

Chief Two Elk arrived to the beating of drums and crackling rattles. As host of the feast, he took his place at the left of the altar rock. He sat grandly on his white horse. His feathered headdress swayed in the breeze.

Most of the adults of the village were assembled, and all of the young men—some standing solemnly, some observing from a distance, smirking. All uninvited girls had found important duties to attend in camp this day.

The drums sounded again. The sun was high in the sky. It was time to begin the sacred ceremony.

Twenty-five girls formed a circle around the altar rock, which had been painted red with bloodroot. On each side of the rock a new arrow was lightly stuck into the ground. Behind the girls the chaperons sat in a circle, each one watching her own girl closely.

Chief Two Elk called each girl from the circle. "Little Heart of the Lodge of Big Heart," the Chief announced first.

Slowly and gracefully, Little Heart left the circle and walked toward the red altar. She declared her purity. She touched first the altar, and then the two arrows. There was a stir among the spectators. Little Heart returned to the circle.

The name of each girl was called, and each girl touched the altar and arrows in the same manner.

"Star Girl of the lodge of Wind Woman."

Star Girl trembled as she took her turn. Would one of the young men challenge her? Would it mean, perhaps, his death? She declared her purity, then touched the red altar.

She saw that the arrows were swaying lightly. Would they fall and disgrace her? "Do not fall, arrows," she whispered.

The arrows did not fall. No voice called. Star Girl walked back to the circle, smiling. She heard the murmur of the spectators, but she saw them only as a blur of color.

Little Heart was called to serve food, and as each girl brought a wooden bowl handed her by the chaperon, Little Heart filled it with food delicacies. The girls ate of the choice food and then returned the bowls to the chaperons.

The drums sounded again, this time more rapidly. "Poom-poom-poom."

It was time for the traditional Maiden's Dance. This was the part Star Girl liked. She had practiced the dance until she could keep in step without thinking.

In low tones the girls chanted the rhythm of their steps. Four times they danced around the red altar, looking like spring flowers tossing in a breeze.

Star Girl had not dared look about her before, but as she danced in her beautiful white dress, she peered into the faces of the crowd. She saw in the blur of color only the smiling face of Norkuk. Her heart danced as lightly as her white moccasins.

Each girl, as she departed from the circle, again touched the altar, vowing to remain pure until she should meet her husband.

The circle broke. There was excited laughter among the girls and relieved sighs from the chaperons. The ceremony had gone smoothly.

Several young men walked directly to their favorite girls and made proposals. The majority, however, eyed their prospects from a distance. They were too timid to break through the ring of chaperons, who still kept a strict eye on their girls.

"Little Heart. Where is Little Heart?" Star Girl asked, looking for her friend. Through the crowd she saw Little Heart in her bright yellow dress and started toward her.

Wind Woman touched her arm, stopping her. Star

Girl turned her head and looked where the grass-root woman nodded. Two tall young men were walking toward her.

Star Girl glanced quickly around, but she and Wind Woman stood alone.

The two young men noticed each other then, and both halted. There was a brief exchange of words, a gesture, and then one turned sharply and walked away.

The victor continued walking toward Star Girl, proudly. It was Norkuk.

The Black Prairie Turnip

When Star Girl was not digging roots, she rode the white pony with Little Heart up and down the grassy knolls and far across the prairie. As often as she could, she visited Norkuk's mother, who was teaching her to quill.

It seemed to Star Girl, however, that she was always digging roots. Wind Woman stayed most of the time in her lodge, rubbing her old aching bones with witch-hazel liniment.

Whenever Star Girl felt she knew every flower in the woods, she saw a new one, peeking from behind a tree stump, or poking its head through tangles of grass. She took each new plant to Wind Woman.

"What is this strange flower, Wind Woman?" Star Girl asked, showing her a tall green flower. Its leaves were waxy green. At the top of the stem were little branches of tiny blossoms, and they too were green.

"There can't be another new flower in the woods already," Wind Woman said, chuckling. She hobbled to the doorway for better light.

113

"Look at its crooked root!" Star Girl said. She held the plant its full length. It reached to her waist.

"I thought you would find it soon," Wind Woman said. "It is deadly poison. It is the Indian poke."

"Oh!" gasped Star Girl. She looked closely at the dark mass of roots.

"Not only is the root poisonous," Wind Woman continued, "but the leaves and the stem and the little green flowers."

"Do you ever use it for medicine, Wind Woman?" Star Girl asked. She held the plant from her, afraid of its power.

"I mix its root with other medicine," Wind Woman said. "It is good for madness and melancholy. But," she warned, "one grain of the root makes a bird fly crazy. Gather the poke carefully."

One day returning to camp with a bag of the powerful Indian poke roots, Star Girl stopped at the edge of the woods to rest. She watched several women digging the red turnip for the evening meal.

She had never dug in the hot sun for food. Every day she dug roots in the woods, but the woods were cool. The woods were filled with pink and yellow flowers. And soft music of little creatures.

Sometimes her back ached, though. She was glad that food would be waiting at the lodge. Wind Woman was given food and clothing for her services. And Norkuk also brought food. Star Girl said the name of Norkuk tenderly, for she was promised to him.

As she thought of Norkuk and watched the women dig the red turnip, she remembered his strange command: "Do not dig the black turnip!"

For a long time Star Girl sat brooding, probing the hisso into the ground at her side. "I will dig the black turnip," she said aloud, rising.

The black turnip was not easily found, however. The coarse, shorter stalks of the red plant were waving at every turn, but the taller stalks of the black turnip were scarce. Whenever Star Girl saw one, there were other women digging about, so she continued walking up and down the knolls until she was far south of the camp.

On the side of a knoll, near the place she had first seen Norkuk, Star Girl finally saw the thick green leaves of a black turnip plant. She looked around cautiously and then ran toward it.

She sank to her knees and began probing the dry earth with the hisso. She looked up every few minutes, furtively, remembering how Norkuk had surprised her before. For what seemed a very long time, Star Girl dug aound the large fleshy root. Dirt flew in all directions.

She stopped to rest for a minute, feeling guilty. Perhaps Norkuk forbade her digging the black turnip only because it was so difficult—and unnecessary. Still, she must know.

Star Girl began digging again. When she felt the root was loosened in its cavity, she began tugging and pulling at it. She pulled with both hands.

The root came out suddenly, and Star Girl fell back with it on the soft dirt. She sat up, brushed the dirt from her face and hair, and looked down at the root as big as her head. It looked like any other prairie turnip she had seen—maybe bigger.

She looked sheepishly around, hoping no one had seen her. Then she stood and brushed the dirt from her dress. "What will I do with it?" she said, trying to lift the big plant. It was too big to carry back to camp with the root bag already filled. She dropped it.

There was something blue in the ground—in the cavity where the root had been! Star Girl dropped to her knees and looked into the deep hole.

Far below she saw high mountains and green valleys. A long river flowed from snow-capped mountains through the green valleys. Near the river were tepees with thin curls of smoke trailing upward. Old men were soaking in pools along the banks of the river, women were carrying water to the tepees, and children and dogs ran in play.

"Ee-dah-how!" Star Girl gasped. *"Ee-dah-how!"*

Far below, a young girl was walking away from the camp toward the marshlands. She walked toward a tall glimmering tree standing apart from other trees. Near the tree was a medicine pile.

The young girl took a stone from her pocket, held it for a minute, then carefully placed it on top of the pile. Then she put her hands over her face as if weeping.

"Only Child," Star Girl exclaimed. "My sister. My home. My people at Hot Springs. My people of the Snake. Wise One, my mother; Tagee, my father."

"Only Child," Star Girl cried. "Only Child, do you hear me?" Star Girl pounded her fists into the warm sod. "I am Star Girl. I am Bannock. Do you hear me, Only Child? Do you hear me?"

Far below, Only Child turned sadly from the tree. She did not hear.

Star Girl wept as she remembered.

A Strange Story

Norkuk galloped his black pony around the camp, around the dusty corrals, and along the edge of the woods looking for Star Girl. Then he turned his pony south toward the prairie knolls, somehow realizing where he would find her.

He slowed his pony to a trot, and then to a walk. Soon he dismounted and led the pony to the black turnip knoll where Star Girl sat.

Star Girl stood defiantly as Norkuk approached. "I am Star Girl, Bannock, daughter of Tagee. Why am I a prisoner here?" she demanded.

"You are not a prisoner," Norkuk said. He walked quickly toward her. "You will understand—"

Star Girl drew back. "Why did you keep this secret from me?" She met Norkuk's gaze, her eyes flashing anger.

Norkuk gestured helplessly. "Do not be angry with me," he said. "You will understand when I tell you. Sit down."

118

Holding the reins of his pony, Norkuk stood in silhouette against the darkening sky. He showed no emotion, but when he spoke his voice was tender.

"We are the Cheyenne of the Sky," Norkuk began, "the stars for your people. Long ago the Great God placed us here to save us from the hands of our enemy. It was so long ago that none of our people remember it, not even Wind Woman."

Star Girl remembered how she had watched the stars at night, pointing with Only Child to the brightest one.

Norkuk continued. "When I was younger, I was once gathering roots and grasses with Wind Woman in the woods. I had wandered a short distance from her to a berry bush by a stream. I heard a whimper. I thought it was the cry of a wounded animal, so I followed the cry.

"I found an old, old woman with a broken leg. She was so old and shrunken that she was no bigger than a child. I called to Wind Woman, and together we set the old woman's leg and carried her to her tree lodge deep in the woods. We stayed with her a night, caring for her.

"She was a grass-root woman, so old she had forgotten her name. But she remembered being trans-

ported to the sky when she was a very young girl. She
told Wind Woman many cures from roots which Wind
Woman had never dug.

"Because I had found her," Norkuk continued, "she
told me the secret of the black turnip." Norkuk pointed
to the plants on the knoll. "She told me the magic to
bring someone from earth up to us through the sky
hole of the black turnip."

Norkuk rubbed the nose of his black pony. Then
avoiding the gaze of Star Girl, he said, "I watched
many nights from the sky hole for someone who
wanted to come."

Star Girl looked up, surprised. "I did not want to

come," she said. She remembered how she had chased the porcupine up the tree, and how Only Child had run back and forth beneath the tall tree, crying.

Then Star Girl remembered something else. She remembered lying outside the tepee at Hot Springs, shivering in the autumn evening and vowing, "I shall marry that star up there." It had been a bright star, she remembered.

Star Girl looked at Norkuk. Could he have been that star?

Norkuk smiled.

There was silence. Then Star Girl asked, "May I return down the poplar tree—the way I came?"

"You may return," Norkuk said, his smile fading, "but with your return the magic ends. You could never come back here."

There was silence again. The black pony whinnied and jerked at the reins. Star Girl probed her fingers into the soft earth.

"Have you not been happy here?" Norkuk asked hopefully.

Star Girl looked down at her feet and watched a tiny ant crawl over her moccasins. It was difficult to be angry with Norkuk. But she could not think of Norkuk now. She could only remember Wise One, little One Arrow, her older brothers, and her new sister, Only Child, who now placed stones on a medicine pile by the tall poplar tree.

"I am Bannock," Star Girl said firmly. "I will return to my people."

Norkuk kneeled and gently touched Star Girl's shoulder. "I want to make you happy here," he said. "I will go hunting—for many days. When I return tell me your final decision, and then I will do as you say."

They walked in silence to the camp, Norkuk leading his pony, Star Girl carrying her root bag. As they approached the camp they heard low wailing cries. They walked quickly toward the lodge of Wind Woman, but stopped when it came in sight. Mourners, like black birds, hovered around the lodge.

Star Girl stood motionless. Then slowly she dropped her root bag to the ground. Norkuk's hand reached for hers.

Through the doorway stepped Doll Man, shaking his rawhide rattle in one hand and clutching his wooden doll in the other. *"Hai yo e yo e-e-yo,"* he cried, dancing back and forth in front of the lodge.

A dark-robed figure approached them from the group of mourners around the lodge. It was Norkuk's mother.

"Grass-root Woman has seen her shadow," The Quiller said sadly. "She is dead."

A Lonely Lodge

Star Girl sat alone in the lodge of Wind Woman as she had for many days. She mourned for Wind Woman and cut her long hair short to show her grief. From kindness she was left alone.

She waited anxiously for Norkuk's return so she might return to her people. She told this to no one, not even Little Heart, who came daily. Each day Little Heart rode her white pony slowly away from the lonely lodge.

Star Girl idly surveyed the heaps of roots to be ground. She touched them, and pushed them aside. "There will be another grass-root woman," she said, "or Doll Man will gladly take them to his lodge." She would forget the roots and her life with Wind Woman. She would return to her people of the Snake.

Again she would run with Only Child, carefree, along the banks of the Portneuf. They would shout and sing so that their voices bounced from the steep canyon walls. She would snuggle with Only Child around big campfires, watching her brothers wrestle, listening to

124

the strange stories of her elders. Remembering, Star Girl buried her head in her hands and wept for her childhood home.

She did not hear the approaching footsteps, so was startled when her name was called.

"Star Girl. Star Girl." It was Norkuk.

Star Girl moved toward the lodge door, but she did not ask Norkuk to enter.

"Star Girl," Norkuk called again. "It is Norkuk. I have returned. I have brought you fur of the red fox."

It was not fur of the red fox that Star Girl wanted. She was silent.

Norkuk waited, but Star Girl gave no answer. Then he asked, "What is your decision, Star Girl?"

"My decision is the same," Star Girl said, her voice sounding strange in the quiet lodge. "I will return to my people."

There was a long silence. Then Norkuk asked hopefully, "Could I—could we not be your people now?"

Star Girl did not answer, but stared at the door of the lodge, blinking tears.

"I will accept your decision as I promised," Norkuk said bravely. After waiting a few minutes he continued, "The moon must be a new moon. Meet me in three nights at the spot where you dug the black turnip. I will be waiting."

He dropped the red fox fur at the lodge door. Soon Star Girl heard his footsteps fade into the distance.

Loud cries awakened Star Girl from a restless sleep.

"Grass-root Woman, Grass-root Woman. Come quickly!"

Star Girl pushed back the door flap and peered through her floppy shorn hair into the gray evening. She saw a young child.

"Follow me, Grass-root Woman. Follow me, Grass-root Woman, with your medicine."

"Grass-root Woman is dead," Star Girl said sharply.

"You are Grass-root Woman now. You come," the girl cried breathlessly.

"Go to Doll Man," Star Girl said, dropping the door flap. "He can cure your sick."

Frightened, the young child backed away from the lodge.

Star Girl felt very much alone. She pulled at her straggly hair, then flung herself on her sleeping mat. She had just dozed again into an unpleasant dream when she heard rapid footsteps and the same tearful voice.

"Grass-root Woman, you must come. It is your friend, Little Heart. She is wounded. She is dying!"

Star Girl jumped to her feet and opened the flap

for the child. "What is it?" she asked anxiously. "What has happened to Little Heart?"

Fitfully the young child told of the accident. The white pony had been running on the prairie and had stepped in a prairie dog's hole. The pony had stumbled, and Little Heart had been hurled to the ground. The pony had returned alone to the camp at dusk, dragging its broken leg. Little Heart now lay unconscious in the lodge of her parents.

Star Girl stared dumbly into the anxious face of the small girl. Then she turned to survey the many root bags hanging from the lodge pole. She was not a grass-root woman. She knew no magic. She could not cure Little Heart.

Grass-root Woman

"Doll Man is singing the spirit of Little Heart to the Great God," the small child cried.

"I will come," Star Girl said.

Her hands felt cold as she gathered medicine bags from the pole. She tried to remember what Wind Woman had taught her—windflower for the wound, blue gentian and pavame for the fever.

"I am ready," she said to the child. They went swiftly into the darkness.

"Help me, Wind Woman," Star Girl whispered as she ran with the child. "Help me to remember what you have taught me. Stay with me, Wind Woman. Stay with me!"

They ran past many lodges in the camp circle, silent and dark with night. Then at the east side of camp they reached the lodge of Big Heart.

Inside the lodge Doll Man danced around the pale, inert form of Little Heart, chanting dolefully and shaking his rawhide rattle. His dancing figure made grotesque shadows on the walls of the lodge.

Little Heart's parents, Big Heart and Fire Bug, sat on the lower bench of the lodge staring into the fire. The small child crept quietly beside them.

"I must work without the medicine man," Star Girl said to Big Heart, remembering the practice of Wind Woman. She kneeled at the side of Little Heart and saw that her friend's arm was bleeding heavily. She pressed a deerskin compound over the wound.

"*Ah-h!*" cried Doll Man, shaking his rattle at Star Girl.

Big Heart rose to his feet and motioned for the medicine man to leave. "She has been taught the magic of Wind Woman. She will stay. Doll Man will go."

Angrily, the medicine man left, but he lingered near the lodge. As Star Girl worked long into the night she could hear his rattle not far away.

"Guide my hands, Wind Woman. Guide my hands," Star Girl whispered as she mixed her medicine.

She cleansed Little Heart's face with witch-hazel liniment, and pressed cold, wet skins to her forehead. She bathed the bruised body in a warm, tansy mixture.

From Wind Woman's medicine bag she took raccoon's grease and gently spread it over the wounds. She applied the powder of the roots—windflower and squawroot. Then she wrapped the wounded areas in soft deerskin.

Soon Little Heart regained consciousness and whimpered from her bed. When the whimpering ceased, Little Heart slept.

For a long time Star Girl watched the sleeping face of her friend. Then her own eyelids became heavy with sleep, and she lay by the side of Little Heart.

Star Girl awoke to the cries of Little Heart. Little Heart's arm was swollen twice its size, and her bruised shoulder was dark and ugly. She tossed her head with pain and fever.

Star Girl kneeled at the side of her friend. What could she do? What would Wind Woman have done? She tried to remember everything the grass-root woman had told her.

She called to Fire Bug, who was still staring into the fire. "I will need more water—cold water from the stream."

Fire Bug roused the small child, who ran quickly with the water paunch.

Again Star Girl bathed the bruised body with a warm tansy mixture. She applied fresh raccoon's grease and more powder to the wounds. She mixed stronger medicine—crooked medicine from the groundcherry root, and sweet medicine from the root of the hop

vine. She held Little Heart's head while she spooned
the pavame tea into her swollen mouth. She packed
the injured arm with cold skins to reduce the swell-
ing.

All day Star Girl worked at the side of Little Heart,
changing the cold skins and applying more medicine.
All day the small child carried cold water from the
stream.

When darkness came, Little Heart slept. The parents
of Little Heart still sat on the lower bench, staring
into the fire. The small child holding the water paunch
fell asleep on her mat. Star Girl sat by the side of her
patient, watching.

The night was long, and Star Girl was afraid. She
was afraid Little Heart would not wake in the morn-

ing. She was afraid Big Heart would say, "You are not Grass-root Woman. You have no magic!"

She wondered if she could remember all that Wind Woman had told her. "It is not magic," Wind Woman had said. "It is knowledge." Had she listened when Wind Woman told her about a medicine that would cure Little Heart? Or had she been thinking of the throwing-stick or the white pony?

Perhaps there was a flower in the woods with roots to cure Little Heart that she did not know—that she would never know. Perhaps the villagers would throw the roots at her and drive her out on the wide prairie. Alone. In the dark.

Star Girl shivered, and waited for morning.

Early in the morning Little Heart opened her eyes and smiled into the anxious face of her nurse.

Star Girl smiled. Tears of joy rolled down her cheeks.

Little Heart asked for water. Then she slept again. Star Girl knew she would be well soon.

Star Girl was very tired, but she was very happy. She looked at the medicine bags near her. "You *are* magic," she said. Then she whispered, "Thank you, Wind Woman. Thank you for staying with me."

The parents of Little Heart embraced Star Girl.

"*Napave* woman, blessed woman," Fire Bug cried. She kneeled and kissed the moccasins of Star Girl.

Big Heart laid beautiful furs and skins at her feet. "My finest furs and my finest colt are yours," he said. "You have saved my daughter. You shall never want."

In the gray of evening Star Girl returned to her lodge. She walked wearily, leading a sorrel pony loaded with gifts. She had saved the life of her friend, and she had received many gifts. She would have been happy without the gifts.

Everywhere were faces smiling at her, hands waving in greeting, and voices whispering proudly, "Grass-root Woman passes."

Star Girl lifted her shoulders and walked proudly. "Now I know who I am," she said. "I am Star Girl, Grass-root Woman of the Cheyenne of the Sky; best friend of the champion Little Heart; favorite of—"

She suddenly remembered. The new moon shone above. Three days had passed. Norkuk was waiting by the black turnip knoll on the prairie.

Star Girl stood a long time looking south across the prairie, wondering. She was proud to be Grass-root Woman. She was happy here. She felt now that she could not return to her childhood home. She would never forget that home, but she could not return.

The sorrel pony became impatient and nuzzled her arm.

"Come along then, little pony," Star Girl whispered, and led it toward her lodge. "You will like your new life with me," she said, patting the pony's nose.

Walking with the pony, Star Girl remembered what her childhood sister had once said, meeting her new life.

> Happily I shall greet the day;
> Proudly I shall walk my way.

"So shall I," Star Girl whispered to the little pony.

Star Girl sat in her lodge, too happy for sleep.

EE-DAH-HOW

Ee-dah-how

In the silver light of dawn a tall young girl climbed down an old poplar tree. She stood timidly on the marshland, adjusting a belt at her waist from which hung assorted plants and roots. Her fringed doeskin dress was scarcely visible under the dangling plants. Heavy braids plaited with fern were coiled about her ears.

Her dark almond eyes surveyed the scene before her: towering mountains tipped with snow, a swift river winding to the west, and beyond the sagebrush and sunflowers, a tepee camp with smoke rising lazily into the sky.

Then she saw the other girl—a short, dark girl with long braids hanging to her knees. She stood motionless in the gray sagebrush.

The tall young girl extended her hand, but the girl in the brush moved backward. Fear showed on her face.

"Hello," the tall girl said. As she moved, the plants swayed against her body.

137

The frightened girl in the brush whispered, "You are Tukuarika?"

The tall girl shook her head.

"Then you are a Nin-num-bee!" The girl with long braids turned and fled through the sagebrush, shouting, "A Nin-num-bee, a Nin-num-bee!"

The tall girl followed her through the brush, stumbling over rocks and tangling her plants. "Wait," she cried, "wait for me."

Her only answer was the plaintive song of little gray birds, "Killdeer, killdeer," and the low lapping of the river.

The chase was short and ended in the middle of the tepee camp. Women in worn robes left their fires and gathered noisily. Men peered from tepee doorways. Dogs barked.

"A Nin-num-bee has swum up the river," the girl with long braids cried. She pointed to the young stranger with the plants, who stood timidly in the circle of women.

The women drew back, frightened. They stared in silence.

One woman stepped out from the group and looked cautiously at the tall girl standing alone. An antelope-tooth necklace hung from the woman's neck. Suddenly she clasped her hands to her face, dropping a basket of currants. "Call Wise One," she gasped.

The women divided noisily, making a path for an old, old woman.

Wise One hobbled into the circle, blinking in the

light of day. Her old head, covered with a doeskin robe, shook in disbelief as she approached the young stranger.

"Star Girl, my child," she whispered. "You have returned. You have returned from the sky." Her voice quavered. Tears fell from her eyes, and she held out her wrinkled arms.

The women gasped, then chattered excitedly.

The tall girl stepped closer to the old woman. "I am Snow Flower," she said, smiling. "I am the daughter of Star Girl, Grass-root Woman." She indicated the plants hanging from her belt. "I have brought plants for medicine."

The old woman, weeping, held the hands of Snow Flower. She touched the heavy, coiled braids and the soft, fringed dress. "My child, my child," she whispered.

The woman who had dropped her basket said to the girl with long braids, "Call Paseego, your father. Call Commosie and One Arrow."

The men stood at a distance, with folded arms. They stared at the young stranger with her curious collection of roots, and then they stared at one another.

Snow Flower wanted to run from these strangers staring at her, grinning at her. But she did not run.

She stood bravely and whispered as she had been taught,

> Happily I shall greet the day;
> Proudly I shall walk my way.

A small child, wakened by the noise, sat up on his mat and rubbed his eyes. "Ee-dah-how," he cried, pointing to the mountains. "Ee-dah-how!"

Snow Flower looked eastward. There was the sun coming down the mountains. It was a beautiful new day.

About the Author

THELMA HATCH WYSS writes: "I wanted Star Girl to be Bannock or Shoshoni because I know the locale of these Indians—southern Idaho. I spent my childhood on a ranch along the banks of the Portneuf River a few miles from the Fort Hall Indian Reservation. In *Star Girl,* Great Falls is Shoshone Falls on the Snake River near the town of Twin Falls, Idaho. Big Camp represents the city of Pocatello, and Hot Springs represents the town of Lava Hot Springs, noted for its natural hot mineral pools.

"Though all my life I have seen the Bannock Indians wandering the country roads in old wagons, hunting squirrels in our fields, and riding broncos at rodeos, I found when I started to write about them that I knew them only as reservation Indians, and therefore, had to research their early customs."

Star Girl is Thelma Hatch Wyss's first book for children.